T0095969

Praise for *Enemy in the Country*

"Theodor Lessing was one of the leading public intellectuals and free spirits of the era from when Germany became a unified country until it became its own enemy, warning of the dangers of freedom and being murdered when the end of that freedom set in. This volume of essays, poems and stories, again in brilliant translation by Peter Appelbaum, is available for the first time in English. The experience of World War I and its aftermath is captured in satire and philosophy signaling the fragile nature of an open public discourse."

> Dr. Frank Mecklenburg
> Mark M. and Lottie Salton Senior Historian
> Director of Research and Chief Archivist
> Leo Baeck Institute

"In his youth, Theodor Lessing (1872-1933) aspired a literary career. Even after establishing himself as a philosopher, he continued writing poems, novellas and stories. He published a number of his prose texts in the collection *Feind im Land* (1923), the title of which refers to the allied occupation of the Rhineland in the aftermath of the First World War. Lessing's collection is beautifully translated by Peter C. Appelbaum."

> Dr. Herman Simissen,
> Open University of the Netherlands
> Author, *Theodor Lessing's Philosophy of History in its Time* (2021)

Enemy
in the
COUNTRY
Satires and Novellas

THEODOR LESSING

Translated and edited by
PETER C. APPELBAUM

BLACK
WIDOW
PRESS

STONE TOWER PRESS

Black Widow Press is an imprint of Commonwealth Books, Inc., Boston MA. Distributed to the trade by NBN (National Book Network) throughout North America, Canada, and the U.K. All Black Widow Books are printed on acid-free paper, and glued into bindings. Black Widow Press and its logo are registered trademarks of Commonwealth Books, Inc.
        Joseph S. Phillips and Susan J. Wood, Ph.D., Publishers.

Stone Tower Press is a Rhode Island corporation. All design, production, and printing is done in the United States.
        Timothy J. Demy, Ph.D., publisher

Cover Art: *Le Petit Journal illustré* 28 January 1923, license obtained from Alamy.com

Formatting and cover design by Amy Cole, JPL Design Solutions

Paperback ISBN: 978-1-7371603-9-7
Printed in the United States
10 9 8 7 6 5 4 3 2 1

*The publication of this work
was made possible by a generous grant from
The Max and Anna Levinson Foundation
and the assistance of Rachel Blackmon
and Jim Kates and Zephyr Press.*

Table of Contents

Introduction

Who is the Real Enemy in the Country?
The Philosophizing Satirist or the Philosopher Inclined to Satire?
Thoughts on Theodor Lessing

Who is the real enemy in the country? The internal or the external one? Theodor Lessing posed this question in his satirically written parable "Enemy in the Country," referring in it to the political conditions at the beginning of the twentieth century. World War I cost the lives of millions of people. The revolution of 1919 and its utopia of a classless society failed—in Lessing's opinion because of the good-naturedness of the downtrodden: "In 1918, the people [...] lost their revolution because they believed more deeply in justice than in power. The proletariat wanted to be just. Just, even to all who believed in nothing and wanted nothing but: Power."[1] A renewed uprising also failed during the *Ruhraufstand* (rebellion in the Ruhr area) of 1920, in which labor rebelled against big business through a general strike.

The rift in German society was deeper than ever, and hopes that accompanied the founding of the Weimar Republic gave way to political lethargy. When the economically important Ruhr region was occupied by French troops in 1923, the government, fueled by big business and the military, tried to exploit the rebellious people to thwart the occupation. The state appealed to the patriotism of the people and demanded unconditional allegiance from the workers. In "Enemy in the Country," labor leader Jens Liebrecht (based on revolutionary leader Karl Liebknecht, who was murdered by the *Freikorps* in 1919 after the failed January Uprising) and industrialist Baldur Tünnes (based on Hugo Stinnes, a major industrialist and influential politician) face each

1

other as negotiating partners. Tünnes, who under other circumstances would never have deigned to accept Liebrecht as an interlocutor, is willing pro forma to ally with labor against the external enemy—but on his terms. Like his peers, he believes that even proletarian leaders "would rather smoke cigars than shed blood" (*Feind im Land,* S. 107, see p. 89 in this translation).

Lessing shows here once again the deep contempt of existing power elites for the people and their spokespersons. They only enter into a short-term alliance of convenience in order to then immediately exploit the human and material resources for their own maintenance of power. Liebrecht's words go unheard in the "Great Hall of the People":

> You always speak of an "enemy in the country!" Yes! We *have*
> an enemy in the country. Around me sit the select leaders of
> our hemisphere, the world's great intellects. [...] all these are
> the country's enemy. (*Feind im Land,* S. 86f., see p. 76f in this
> translation).

Theodor Lessing was also considered an enemy in the country in right-wing circles, and not just since the National Socialists came to power. Exactly seven months after Adolf Hitler took office, he was assassinated in exile. At the end of February 1933, Theodor Lessing decided to leave Germany, hoping to be safe from the Nazis in Prague. The very night Lessing fled, an SA squad entered his Hanover home and smashed the furniture. In a letter that Lessing wrote to a family friend immediately after his escape, he says:

> For us, too, the times have brought many difficulties, above all
> the necessity of fleeing across the German border. In the last few
> weeks I was constantly subjected to harassment and threats and,
> as one of the ostracized "Communists," "Marxists," and "traitors
> of the people," subjected to protective custody. So I fled across the
> border in time.[2]

Lessing had been under close observation since his arrival in Prague. Four days before he was murdered, agents of the Gestapo reported from the café of the Prague Parliament at the Charles Tower: "Well, Mr. Einstein is not there, but there sits Professor Theodor Lessing, who escaped from Germany in time and recently opened an ideological department store in front of the astonished Prague people, in which he declared that he was 'Jew, Zionist, German, Communist and Socialist at the same time.'"[3]

Two days after Lessing's murder (30 August, 1933), the *Niederdeutsche Zeitung*, published in his hometown of Hanover, gloatingly reported: "Now this unholy spook is also wiped away."[4] Thomas Mann noted in his diary: "I dread such an end, not because it is the end, but because it is so miserable and may suit a Lessing, but not me."[5] It remains to be asked what made this thinker seem so dangerous in the eyes of the Nazis that he was the first "traitor to the people" to be liquidated abroad. Joseph Goebbels, who approved the bounty for Lessing's murder, declared at the Nuremberg party congress on September 2, 1933, that it was not surprising that "the German revolution" would now also bring "the shaking off of this yoke"—he referred, among others, to Theodor Lessing, who had been murdered two days earlier.

Despite or perhaps because of this ominous fate, Theodor Lessing the thinker and the victim has since been largely forgotten. It is only through the re-publication of some of his writings in the early 1980s that he has once again come to the attention of both historians and philosophers. The present translation of his satire *Feind im Land*, published in 1923, helps make this visionary and pugnacious thinker accessible to a wider readership. In order to be able to assess Theodor Lessing's manifold talents and complex thought processes, his career is briefly outlined.

After studying medicine and psychology in Freiburg, Bonn and Munich, Lessing received his doctorate in philosophy in Erlangen. In 1900 he married the noblewoman Maria Stach von Goltzheim. Between 1901 and 1904 he worked as a reform pedagogue in the rural educational homes of Haubinda and Laubegast. In 1906 he resumed his studies, first with Edmund Husserl in Göttingen, then in his native

Hanover, where he habilitated in 1907 with the paper *Der Bruch in der Ethik Kants* (The Breach in the Ethics of Kant) at the Technical University of Hanover. In 1908 he received a position as associate professor of philosophy there. During World War I, he worked as a military doctor and wrote the two books *Philosophie als Tat* and *Europa und Asien* (Philosophy as an Act and Europe and Asia).[6] The latter was banned by the military censors when it appeared in 1918 and could not appear in 1919. In his main philosophical work with the programmatic title *Geschichte als Sinngebung des Sinnlosen*, (History as Making Sense of the Senseless) which was published a year later,[7] Lessing discussed the sense or nonsense of historiography.

The main conclusion of the above work is:

> *Denkt man vollendete "Rationalität" (d.h. Herrschaft der Vernunft und Vernunftgebote) als Ziel der Geschichte, so erwäge man wohl, ob nicht das Logische auch das "Tote" und das Lebendige eben darum Leben ist, weil es noch "nicht" Vernunft ward.* [If one thinks of completed "rationality" (i.e., rule of reason and the laws of reason) as the goal of history, one should consider whether the logical is not also the "dead" and the living is not life precisely because it has not yet become reason].

In this work, Lessing came to the sobering conclusion that history reflected neither life nor truth, but that it was above all not a science. History, in the sense of historical tradition, was rather a myth. During his lifetime, however, Theodor Lessing attracted less attention as a philosopher—it was not until 1922 that he received a non-tenured associate professorship at the University of Hanover—than as an essayist and political journalist. Two affairs in particular brought him to the attention of everyone and fatefully determined his life: the Haarmann case (1924) and Lessing's anti-Hindenburg article (1925). As an accredited correspondent, Theodor Lessing had taken part in the spectacular trial of mass murderer Fritz Haarmann in 1924. Both as a journalist and as a psychologist and cultural critic, he followed the course of the trial from the very beginning. The defense even considered using Lessing as a psychological expert witness in the trial of the mass murderer. Erich Frey, Haarmann's first public defender, asked Lessing for an assessment, since he was, in his opinion, very familiar with the case. However, when Frey resigned his mandate, the new public defender refused an expert witness, saying, "I wouldn't know what to ask for psychologically." Lessing —who had already expressed to Frey that he saw in the Haarmann phenomenon a mirror of society: "I actually mean the guilt that affects us all, our entire culture, our social order [...]"—now put his assessments up for public discussion in his articles about the spectacular trial. This met with such suspicion from the public prosecutor's office, that he was excluded from the trial on the eleventh day of the hearing. The reason given was terse: "We cannot tolerate a gentleman in the courtroom who practices psychology." Nevertheless, Lessing continued to follow the court proceedings and wrote about them in the local and national press. In his articles, he attacked the entire judiciary: the prosecution, the jury, and the defense. For him, the Haarmann trial was not just the tribunal against a murderer. Rather, in his view, the Haarmann phenomenon reflected the immorality and social climate of German society as a whole, which had made such a phenomenon possible in the first place. When the proven twenty four-time murderer was sentenced to death, Lessing suggested that the executed man's bones be buried in a public square in Hanover and that a tombstone be erected with the words "Our communal guilt."[8] The public was horrified. Lessing was declared a non-person and socially ostracized.

Another affair that made Lessing famous and infamous in equal measure proved to be more momentous. The stumbling block was an article that Lessing had written on the occasion of the nomination of Field Marshal von Hindenburg as a candidate for the Reich presidency. Lessing had published the article on 25 April 1925, in the *Prager Tagblatt*, a liberal German-language newspaper for which he wrote regularly. On 7 May 1925, an abridged reprint of his Hindenburg portrait appeared in the *Hannoverscher Kurier*, triggering a furious smear campaign against

Lessing. Almost prophetically from today's perspective, Lessing wrote at the end of the article:[9]

> *Nach Plato sollen die Philosophen Führer der Völker sein. Ein Philosoph würde mit Hindenburg nun eben nicht den Thronstuhl besteigen. Nur ein repräsentatives Symbol, ein Fragezeichen, ein Zero. Man kann sagen:"Besser ein Zero als ein Nero." Leider zeigt die Geschichte, dass hinter einem Zero immer ein künftiger Nero verborgen steht.* [According to Plato, philosophers are supposed to be leaders of nations. Hindenburg would not ascend the throne chair as a philosopher, but only as a representative symbol, a question mark, a zero. One can say: "Better a Zero than a Nero." Unfortunately, history shows that behind a Zero there is always a future Nero].

Fundamental to Theodor Lessing's thinking is the practical principle of need and its prevention. In the undeniable fact of necessity, human needs, longings, economic hardship, as well as human pain, political oppression and social suffering are expressed. Thus his philosophy is one of necessity and of action. Here lies also his difference with Schopenhauer, who sees escape possibilities from suffering only in art, pity, or resignation.

For Lessing, this idea of the necessity of a reversal in need is not pure idealism; the needs must be recognized and named again and again in the changing times. He is concerned with a political awareness of socially conditioned need. Necessity becomes history. With his philosophy of history, Lessing criticizes historiography as myth-making per se in his book *Geschichte als Sinngebung des Sinnlosen* with precarious consequences up to and including wars.

Always accompanied by the hardship of his own intellectual existence, Lessing published numerous articles and books, among them also a paper on Nietzsche, with whom he felt a kindred spirit and nature. Tireless and fearless, sarcastic and bitter, he analyzed the irrational political forces and interests of his time, commented critically on the currents of philosophy, fought against fascism, and vehemently advocated the preservation of democratic freedoms and fundamental rights, as well as the equality of women and peaceful understanding among peoples. Theodor Lessing made excellent use of the "short forms" of essays, feuilletons and satires as weapons of criticism. If one wants to understand Lessing's thinking, one finds it precisely in these numerous short publications, including the ones in this volume. Lessing's pronounced sense of justice and his democratic understanding can certainly be traced back to his own experience as a Jew and thus as an outsider. "It was my nature to feel I belonged more where I was more needed." Thus Lessing always felt a sense of being drawn to social outsiders.

The image of Theodor Lessing remains ambivalent to this day. However, his writings have lost none of their topicality, as is shown not least by his collection of texts *Enemy in the Country*.

Dr. Elke-Vera Kotowski
Moses Mendelssohn Center for European-Jewish Studies
University of Potsdam

Endnotes

1   Theodor Lessing, "Macht und Recht" in: *Aufruf. Streitschrift für Menschenrechte / Liga für Menschenrechte in der Tschechoslowakei*, vol. 3 (1933), no. 8/9.

2   Letter from Theodor Lessing to Bontjes van Beek Family, Fischerhude, dated March 8, 1933 [private archive Bontjes van Beek, Fischerhude].

3   *Völkischer Beobachter*, August 27/28, 1933.

4   *Niederdeutsche Zeitung*, September 1, 1933.

5   *Thomas Mann, 1933–1934* (Frankfurt am Main: S. Fischer, 1977), 165.

6   Theodor Lessing, *Philosophie als Tat* (Göttingen: Otto Harpe Verlag, 1914); idem, *Europa und Asien* (Berlin: Verlag der Wochenschrift die Aktion, 1918).

7   Idem., *Geschichte als Sinngebung des Sinnlosen* (Munich: C.H. Beck, 1919).

8   Idem., *Haarmann: die Geschichte eines Werwolfs* (Berlin: Die Schmiede, 1925).

9   Idem., "Hindenburg," in: *Prager Tagblatt*, no. 97, April 25, 1925, p. 3; shortened and distorted article in: *Hannoverscher Kurier*, March 7, 1925, quoted from: Rainer Marwedel, *Theodor Lessing (1872–1933). Eine Biographie* (Darmstadt: Hermann Luchterhand, 1987), 259.

Translator's Introduction

Translation and editing any work by Theodor Lessing is a daunting task. As if on purpose, his German is opaque, long-winded, and full of complex words, some (such as *bewußtseinsgehäusedurchbrechend*) almost ridiculously so. Words are made up at will (a peculiarity of the German language). Nouns are often qualified by a long series of adjectives, some of which differ in subtle ways difficult to represent in English; so too use of philosophical terms such as *Ich, Du, Sein, Sosein, Dasein*, and *Werden*. Wordplay is common (*leben, lebendig, lebig, lebevoll; Sinn, Unsinn, Wahnsinn; schauen, anschauen*) and likewise difficult to translate effectively. The reader sometimes gets the impression that Lessing is playing a joke on them, making it difficult to figure out exactly what he is saying. His erudition is great, running the gamut of languages such as Latin and French, combined with a deep knowledge of philosophy.

Lessing's post-war philosophical writings obscure the fact that he worked as a physician in the German Army throughout the war. Although he had not yet sat for his final examinations, his education was complete. He had a very biting tongue, with little good to say about anyone. His statement that Hindenburg was a zero, and that a zero could easily become a Nero, made him many enemies. He was such a perceived threat that a group of Sudeten Germans was specially dispatched to murder him in his study in Marienbad Czechoslovakia on 30 August, 1933, where he had fled soon after Hitler became chancellor on 30 January seven months earlier.

This book of short stories, satires, and novellas (with a poem for added spice)[1] is, far as I can see, unique in Lessing's writings It also contains the only stories he wrote describing his war service. Although he was born Jewish, he converted, but that did not stop him from commenting acerbically on and about fellow-Jews. His book on *Jewish Self-Hate*, published in 1930 is a classic of its kind, containing uncomfortable truths that are valid to this day.[2]

The first two sections are very short. A brief dialogue between a man and a woman on satire and reality is followed by a poem about the 1923 Ruhr occupation by the French, which created great bitterness in Germany and precipitated growth of right wing nationalism. It contains powerful warnings, 10 years before Adolf Hitler became chancellor, on the dangers of threatening a prostrate post-war Germany with reparations and occupation. If the sleeping beast is awakened, results will be dire. The reader is referred to a similar prophetic message by Heinrich Heine.[3]

A novella entitled "Enemy in the Country!" takes up most of this book. It is set during the 1923 French occupation of the Ruhr at the Great Hall of the People in the fictitious town of Dollarcamp, where the occupying French and the Germans are negotiating post-war compensation. Lessing treats us to a panoply of characters, most with acerbically mocking names which I have attempted, where possible, to translate with a Dickensian touch. On the French side there is the comic opera Marshal Boche de Trocadero and his wily Talleyrand-like advisor Faussecocheur. German negotiators include the portly Reich President Guschen Ehrlich, Chancellor Kuno Reißer, industrialists Tünnes and Coalkrupp, War Minister von Fungusbeard, and representatives Baron von Soonwillhave, and Count Klingaling.

Thomas and Heinrich Mann (Manny Shakespeare and Cry-Baby, respectively) are viciously portrayed. Lessing had attacked the now-largely forgotten Prussian Jewish critic Samuel Lublinski for "selling himself to the German literary establishment." Part of that establishment, the novelist Thomas Mann, whose work had been lauded by Lublinski, then published a 1910 article stating that Lessing was a "disgraceful dwarf who should consider himself lucky that the sun shines on him, too." The Lessing Mann affair (*Die Affäre Dr. Lessing*) was the subject of biting exchanges between the two men in 1910 issues of *Die Schaubühne* and *Literarisches Echo*. In a 1910 pamphlet, Lessing referred to Mann as *Tomi die Moralkuh* [Tomi the moral cow].[4] It is not clear what Lessing had against Heinrich Mann, possibly guilt by association.

The Communists send Jens Liebrecht, son of a poor mining family, as their representative. Everyone is manipulated by the wily Jewish banker Mannheimer from Mandelsüß and Company who sits in the corner like an eminence grise, spitting numbers into a telephone and manipulating the markets. There is a great deal of toing and froing, including verbose hypocritical speeches which mean mostly nothing, from both sides. Liebrecht finally threatens the assembly with a bomb if his demands that the French leave are not met, and is beaten half to death. The novella ends with a disillusioned and dying Liebrecht, and nothing really changing. The rich and powerful get richer and more powerful, the working man loses, and Mannheimer makes a great deal of money. Like the poem, this is a work of warning, published before the events actually took place.

In "Comrade Levy," Lessing describes a young Jewish man who volunteers, ostensibly to ease the burden of service. He is the exact opposite of a German soldier: an anti-hero with anxious, faded face, bandy legs, undisciplined, avoiding drill and exercise at every opportunity, slouching, and carrying an inexhaustible supply of gum drops in his pocket. He is an endless source of military and genealogical history, and understands the minutiae of classical sculpture, paintings and tapestries, but balks at the sight of violence and death. And yet, he is shot and killed in the act of putting a dying horse out of its misery. Interestingly, Lessing gives a first-hand account of Belgian *francs-tireurs*, and is not bothered by German looting of civilian property.

The second war story, "Episode," is one of the most powerful I have read. It is a miniature of the 1914 Christmas truce. In 1916, an exhausted German trench unit in La Varennes, France notices a wounded poilu, with a bloodied, half shot away arm, waving at them. They see a wounded German comrade trying to crawl towards them, helped to safety in the German trench by the limping, wounded Frenchman. This gives rise to a brief period of fraternization. Frenchmen and Germans emerge from their trenches and are surprised to see that, underneath the layers of dirt, they are all the same They find common civilian professions, and are soon swopping family photographs and smoking material. The Frenchman is awarded the Iron Cross, and both wounded men are transported to the rear for treatment. Dusk falls, the Germans attack, and are decimated. At the end, a rumor circulates that the image of a wounded man looking like the Frenchman, with a crown of thorns on his head, has been seen limping on the battlefield.

The last chapter, "Prisoner's Greetings," is very difficult. Lessing takes a pressed spring flower sent to him from a Bavarian jail by Gustav Klingelhöfer and Ernst Toller, and muses over the myth of the blue flower, much in vogue during the German Romantic period. This chapter touches on Lessing's view on the anthropomorphism of flowers which is the subject of a separate book.[5]

"Comrade Levi" was written in 1914 and "Episode" in 1916, but their publication was banned by the war censor. "Prisoner's Greeting" was published in abridged form in 1923, in the *Prager Tagblatt*. As stated, these are the only two published war stories by Lessing of which I am aware, and this is the first English translation of this book.

I thank Elke-Vera Kotowski for gracing my translation with an introduction and Tim Demy for making me aware of a neglected treasure and agreeing to publish it. James Scott provided invaluable and essential help with recondite and complex words and sentences, interpretation of exactly whom Lessing was referring to with his nicknames and poetry translation. As always, his assistance was indispensable. Finally, and as always, I thank my wife Addie and daughter Madeleine for putting up with me. All errors are mine alone.

Peter Appelbaum
Land O Lakes, FL
January 2022

Endnotes

1   Theodor Lessing, *Feind im Land. Satiren und Novellen* (Hannover: Wolf Albrecht Adam Verlag, 1923).

2   Idem., *Der jüdische Selbsthaß* (Berlin: Zionistischer-Bücherverband [Jüdischer Verlag], 1930). Idem., *Jewish Self-Hate*, trans. and ed. Peter C. Appelbaum and Benton M. Arnovitz (New York and Oxford Berghahn Books, 2021).

3   See Lewis Browne (ed.), *The Wisdom of Israel* (London: Michael Joseph, 1960), 486–488.

4   Thomas Mann: "Der Doktor Lessing. Ein Pamphlet" *Literarisches Echo*, 1 March 1910; Theodor Lessing. *Samuel Zieht die Bilanz und Tomi melkt die Moralkuh oder Zweier Könige Sturz. Eine Warnung für Deutsche, Satiren zu schreiben* (Hannover: Verlag des "Antirüpel," 1910), 28–44; Thomas Mann, *Das Leben des deutschen Schriftsteller Thomas Mann* (Frankfurt am Main: S. Fischer Verlag, 1975) 821–834; Jacques Darmaund, "Thomas Manns Polemik mit Theodor Lessing," *Germanica* 60, 2017, 167–177.

5   Theodor Lessing, *Blumen* (Berlin: Oesterheld & Co. Verlag, 1928).

1

Conversation[1]

Under the firs of the Deister;[2] July day, man and woman

THE WOMAN: Pfui! You skulk into Aphrodite's sanctuary, and draw a beard under her nose with a piece of coal.

THE MAN: All life is sacred, but I must have the freedom to laugh at everything.

THE WOMAN: Secret tears.

THE MAN: Dearest woman, caricatures do not reflect *reality*. What do I care about real people or real history? If we seek the *truth*, we must stand outside it. Leave me alone to love and hate as I please. It is our nature to hate and love, and judge ourselves as well as others.

THE WOMAN: Your truth will then be *your* reality. People will say that you make those who aspire with you into sacrifices of your own envy and wickedness.

THE MAN: Do I need to explain to you that *all* satire uses reality as a banner? That real contemporaries are nothing more than *random provocations* for its timeless truths? Must I say that real people are only involved insofar as satire *must* have something concrete to anchor it. Do I have to say that I appreciate the *greatness* of all these men

(Ebert, Kuno, Stinnes, Foch, Kayserlinck, Spengler, Scheler, Harden, Ehrhardt, etc.) very well?[3] Would I even bother to take it up with them if they were insignificant?

THE WOMAN: You will have to pay for hurting others.

THE MAN: I don't *want* to hurt anyone. I am very strict with myself. *La taquinerie est la mechanceté des bons.*[4]

THE WOMAN: You prove that you're taking out your anger on others in two ways: You take the mickey out of the Mann brothers[5] and mock university philosophers. Is that not pure bile on your part?

THE MAN: Yes, that's true. My life is wounded, and complicated by contempt, slander, displacement, mistaken identification, almost oppression. But when someone retaliates against me, is it not my fair right to fight back? The mere fact that I have the freedom to do so is my life's purpose.

THE WOMAN: Nobody will understand or believe this.

THE MAN: That's fine with me. I just want one thing. When I sharpen the damascene blade of logic, please don't scream for the police and fight against me with a dung-smeared pitchfork. Use *honest* weapons.

THE WOMAN: I am afraid for you.

THE MAN: I believe in greatness.

Endnotes

1   Theodor Lessing, *Feind im Land. Satiren und Novellen* (Hannover: Wolf Albrecht
     Adam Verlag, 1923), 5–6.

2   A chain of hills in the German state of Lower Saxony, about 25 kilometers south-
     west of the city of Hanover.

3   Friedrich Ebert (1871–1925), German politician of the German Social
     Democratic Party (SPD) and the first president of the Weimar Republic ; Kuno
     von Westarp (1864–1945), conservative German politician during the Weimar
     Republic; Hugo Stinnes (1870–1924), German industrialist and politician;
     Ferdinand Foch (1851–1929), French general and military theorist who served
     as Supreme Allied Commander during World War I; Hermann von Keyserling
     (1880–1946), German social philosopher; Oswald Spengler (1880–1936),
     German historian and history philosopher; Max Scheler (1874–1928), German
     philosopher known for his work in phenomenology, ethics, and philosophical
     anthropology; Maximilian Harden (Felix Ernst Witkowski)(1861–1927), influ-
     ential German journalist and editor. Described at length in Theodor Lessing, *Der
     Jüdische Selbsthass* (Berlin: Jüdischer Verlag, 1930), 167–210 (Idem., *Jewish Self-
     Hate*, trans. and ed. by Peter C. Appelbaum and Benton Arnovitz [New York and
     Oxford: Berghahn Books, 2021]),115–140; Hermann Ehrhardt (1881–1971),
     German Freikorps commander during the period of turmoil in the Weimar
     Republic from 1918 to 1920. Lessing is being sarcastic. The men he cites come
     from many different backgrounds.

4   Victor Hugo (1802–1885). Teasing is the mischievousness of good people.

5   Thomas and Heinrich Mann (see chapter 3, notes 19, 21, 53).

2

Greetings to Barbusse[1]

On the Occupation of the Ruhr, 1922[2]

In the grey of my Hanover's birches[3] and heathland
Heavy with sleep, and yet missing its blessing
Knocked on the lead-covered door of my suff'ring
Song of a young soul, a song come from France.
"I" it said, "bring you the light of Provençe,
Air that's from Paris, the banks of the Seine.
Hail from *la belle*, hail from *la France.*
Courage, friend!"

And I took it to heart from the table now empty
Broke piously bread…And then clattered a sword,
Fire entered, cheering, the land so dishonored.
Since my son fell and ashes my hearth…
Back then in your bloody August's rough dances
I hung bereft on the cross of all pain
While you were handing out victor's laurels.
I said: "No!"

But the day came (you know it, Barbusse)—they were crawling
Out of their graves in the rusty red field.
Souls now defiled with all their bones broken,
English they, Russian they, joined with the French,
Joined now in death, and from their dying mouths
Only one name, of a German, "Karl Liebknecht," emerged.[4]
We then kissed each other and swore all as one:
"No more war!"

Is the heart then so tight that proximate peoples
The Vosges or the Rhine or North Sea can divide?
Are there not world around songs of those spirits
Steeped in the stuff of our cosmic creation?
No more to speak yet of guilt or of debtors,
This we have sworn and with patient forbearance
Each one would carry for each of the others
All the guilt.

Yes, we have sworn it, Barbusse, since we're souls,
Droplets of blood of the peoples we are,
That they might be able to choose their own homeland
When the spider of power spins hair shirts for them –
Should once more that terrible pendulum swing:
You today? Us tomorrow? For each generation?
Should once more the hag ethnic purity sing:
"Might before right?"

Woe! Now yet again the gullible masses
Don the rapacious kit of the soldier
Once more those sickened on sickening hate
Wrap all their haggling schemes in God's will.
For iron and for coal the hagglers of Europe
"Fatherland" cry, they cry "Race" and cry "Prayer,"
Just when they sell to their small band of cronies
You, you rube!

From the Niederwald Germany's Valkyries stare
Angrily down on the Rhine as it rolls,
That it may stir up the youth to revenge.
The hills above Bingen are covered with vines.
The river rolls blood from the hearts of these strangers,
Germany's grapes suck a poisonous brew,
Miserly to the last penny and shift:
Hate on Hate!

But just stop!…The air that your rifles would now split asunder
Nourished Gottfried's heart, slaked Wolfram's thirst.[5]
Mothers here tell their sons you are the foe,
Lorelei pulls your ships down to the deep.[6]
German Masters scorn what is simple, straightforward,
German Kaisers watch over hill and vale,
Take your shoes off! The air we breathe still holds
Goethe's song.[7]

Our cities with arches and spiraling stairways
They hold Holbein's cradle, Beethoven's grave.[8]
Our mighty cathedrals of Mainz and Cologne
Lift threatening fingers into the air.
They warn you: Fear the invisible powers,
They will not suffer your foolishness long
Before they devour the good and the bad
In no time.

Now the blood from our common wounds knits us together
Love does not know what's right, love has no charge.
Brothers before, now again reunited
We will lead all the condemned to the light.
And if you would waken the slumbering monster
It soon will lay waste to the burgeoning fields,
First go the strong, then go the weak,
You will pay!

I look far afield…in empires forgotten
Freeze wasted woods, home to hungering wolves,
The stony cadavers of once famous cities
Sank from swamp to swamp and from mire to mire.
Here's to old Europe's historical days,
Where once the Caucasian Braggart held sway[9]
Till one of the brothers his brother had slain.
Dead lies Death!

Endnotes

1 Theodor Lessing, *Feind im Land. Satiren und Novellen* (Hannover: Wolf Albrecht Adam Verlag, 1923), 7–10; Henri Barbusse (1873–1935), French novelist and a member of the French Communist Party

2 This actually happened in January 1923 (see chapter 3, note 1). The connection to Henri Barbusse is unclear. The poem, written 10 years before Hitler' access to power, contains terrible prophecies of things to come.

3 Lessing was born in Hanover.

4 Karl Liebknecht (1871–1919), German socialist, originally in the Social Democratic Party of Germany (SPD) and later co-founder with Rosa Luxemburg (1871–1919) of the Spartacist League and Communist Party of Germany. Liebknecht and Luxemburg were murdered in 1919 by *Freikorps* members.

5 Many historical personages are possible.

6 A high, steep slate rock on the right bank of the River Rhine, where according to Clemens Brentano (1778–1842) and Heinrich Heine (1897–1856), an enchanting female lures sailors to their death.

7 Johann Wolfgang von Goethe (1749–1832), one of the greatest of all German writers: he was a statesman, scientist, and author of *Faust*.

8 Hans Holbein the Younger (c. 1497–1543), German painter and printmaker; Ludwig van Beethoven (1770–1827), German composer and pianist, one of the greatest composers in the history of Western music.

9 Reference unclear. Substitution of Caucasian with Corsican would have meant Napoleon I.

3

Enemy in the Country! 1923[1]

The sirens shrieked for three long hours during that harsh May month, carrying the news into the gloomy night of potholes and ditches: "The French occupation army is marching on Dollarcamp, to make us pay compensation with money that our oppressed country doesn't have."

The republic's flag waved darkly in the distance over the huge vault of the Great Hall of the People, endowed by the rich old iron and steel magnate Tünnes.[2] A black mass of comrades, armed only with hoes and axes, rose out of the dreary cellars into the grey light of day, gathering on the plain in their hundreds of thousands. Wives and children, old men, unemployed, cripples without number, and the sick from the lost war awaited them there. They stood dumbly like viewers at a funeral near a copse of trees whose leaves had been blown off by an icy wind.

A signal was heard from the distant Ruhr, where the blue river broke through the smoke-covered hillside. Marshall Boche de Trocadero, "Iron Hero of Fatinitza," was coming![3] His infantry was commanded to draw a three-hour- travel wide cordon around Dollarcamp, so that large mortars, braced by the forested hills, could draw a bead on the defenseless rabble. The only road left open to the Great Hall was through the north, because the French knew that the decisive meeting would be held there, and that the tyrannical Treaty of Falfiloques,[4] laid down by statesmen from both sides, would be debated again. While the flower of Europe's intelligentsia waited for the mar-shal's grand entrance under the giant vault, outside in the grey morn-ing mist the gloomy proletarian masses, dull and dumb, stood wedged between rows of threatening artillery on the nearby hills, unaware that the slowly advancing troops had already surrounded them. They had been standing there since 6.00 a.m., waiting for someone to tell them what to do, damned to uncomprehending powerlessness. But they still glowed with national pride. If they got out of control, could the Marshal's bayonets restrain them?

"Let Tünnes speak! Let him speak!" went from mouth to mouth. "Baldur, the Younger, not the Elder."[5]

There he stood on the upper step of the outer staircase at the back of the Great Hall under the Great Balcony, overlooking the plain. Everyone outside could see him. They were the offspring of untold mil-lions of farmers and workers, manipulated by the plutocratic classes, who had ordered them to climb into this same clump of soil, descending generation after generation to bloody death and destruction in the vain hope of conquering first Europe, then the entire civilized world. There he stood—young, broad, blond, healthy, well groomed, a perfect man amongst all this misery! He pointed to the grey spring skies and began.

"Brothers!" You know that our battle against half the world has ended in defeat. You know that they have oppressed us with the scandal-ous Treaty of Falsiloques.[6] We can't pay the tribute that has been forced on us, and now they are coming for our black earth: our coal, our ore. I know: capitalism and labor are enemies—no bridge can connect the haves and the have-nots. But I extend my pleading hand to you. You are like the nearby buds of the forest, outstretched and ready to bloom: let us be *brothers!*"

His arm pointed desperately to the sky, his strong young body trembled, and words choked in his throat.

A pale, dark-eyed young man bounded up the stairs, flickering like a dark narrow, flame against the handsome, blond man. With a single symbolic, all embracing gesture, he grasped Tünnes's right hand and placed the other arm around his neck: "Brother!"

Men strained their heads to see, women raised their children up—
all wanted to see the miracle. It really was a miracle! The head of the
German National Party[7] and Jens Liebrecht, Communist Prophet, had
joined hands.[8] Liebrecht did not yet reveal the entire sordid issue to
the masses.

The blond man hesitated.

Was this a Communist chess gambit?

The question came hesitatingly: "Do you love the homeland
that much?"

"Yes, I do love it."

"You are a good fellow" said the blond man.

"No, *you* are!" said the dark-eyed man.

The watery early spring sun shone over the field, blessing the land
and its children, and the song "Yes, we love, we love our country" rose
to heaven from voices of a hundred thousand people tested in the fires
of war and misery.

In the meanwhile, French infantry and artillery had completed
their encirclement of Dollarcamp along the forested hills. But when
they approached and saw the faces of the massed workers, aflame with
patriotism, they stopped, took up positions and called out: "Stay calm,
comrades! We won't shoot! *We too* are members of the proletariat!"

The workers laughed. A single word, like a holy oath, flew from
mouth to mouth: *General strike.*

Marshal Boche de Trocadero ceremoniously opened the world-historical[9] tragedy in the Great Vault of the People.

Resplendent in his uniform encrusted with gold braid and fifty
different gleaming medals and decorations, his brave old soldier's heart
rejoiced. Now he had them all together under his iron thumb! Lined up in
leather club chairs, there they sat meekly, like obedient army recruits ready
for his orders—Germany's famed windbags, braggarts, scriveners, couch
potatoes, writers, merchants, mathematicians, hagglers, and theoreticians!

What a miserable civilian rabble they were!

The parliamentarians sat in two rows across from each another,
filling the hall like obedient young men at a school prayer meeting.

Their teacher sat before them on a platform, like the president of the Reichstag before his fellow members.

The speaker's platform stood in the middle of the platform. In front of it, the marshal's negotiating table was covered with ornate green baize.

The hall was comfortably heated, and large electric bulbs glowed in the morning half-light. But, at the same time, a ray of May sun flooded through into the murky window from the bare plain.

Faussecocheur, the Talleyrand of our time, sat next to the marshal.[10]

His foxy, smile-wreathed face poked into the marshal's ear, dripping poisonous remarks about the names and profiles of the restless patriots sitting around and making notes.

"Please take note, Monsieur le Maréchal, of that small murky figure. He is Tünnes the Elder, the richest man in the country."

Marshal Boche looked into a pair of dark, melancholy, furtive eyes. They reminded him of Michelangelo's face. Where had he seen that before?[11] At the time, they reminded him of the glittering eyes of a black jaguar ready to pounce.

"The well-groomed gentleman beside him," Faussecocheur continued, "is the famous Herr Coalkrupp:[12] A Prussian guard lieutenant without prejudices (rare in his social class). His profession is that of permanent son-in-law and his wife comes from a long line of royalist senior government and district administrators with too many daughters. No means but great title. Right opposite him sits the blond, fat Thiessen,[13] who is called Cannon Thiessen, the Great Bomb in his intimate circle. Heavy caliber, complicated family tree, but prone to colic. A real hand-on-heart patriot. It's the old, old game:[14] behind everything we find the large banking and financial interests! Habestein, Gewinner, Plutusssohn, Gould,[15] gulden, francs, marks, reals, dollars, pounds— every conceivable type of convertible currency."

A Golden Chair of Honor had been installed opposite the marshal's chair in the first row of the parterre. Sunk into in it was the pumped up gaseous mass, ensconced in a blue frock coat, of the Reich President, whose ponderous task it was to represent the worn out fatherland with his 200 lb. avoirdupois. State officials, dignitaries, political and party leaders sat in serried rows behind his throne, like poor sinners risen out of the grave in the Valley of Jehoshaphat, when the trumpet sounds for the Last Judgment.[16]

Marshall Boche's heart swelled with pride. Here he was king, in loco dei. When his all-seeing, Napoleonic eye wandered over the poor sinners' heads, oh how his conquering valiant heart rejoiced! How he had gotten used to such victories! In the uppermost cozy velvet nest which had always gloried under the name "Imperial Lodge," primped up ladies inspected the world through lorgnettes. Oh, how they hated— and loved!—what they saw.

A hall of mirrors lined the Great Vault of the People.[17]

Artificial electric light reflected onto the glass-covered walls and noble tribunes sitting in the hall—living mirrors and brief chroniclers of our times, "representatives of *Kultur*."[18] Authors, scholars, poets, and heaven knows who else. They sat like apostils, documenting the World Spirit on the margins of history. No! Rather like spectral lights on a black background. They strung themselves together like threatening hieroglyphics, which Boche's simple soldier's heart was incapable of interpreting.

The long, regular row of mystic hieroglyphics was broken on the left side by a towering thin, decadent exclamation mark. He was the poet Männe, Shakespeare of the luxury sanatoria.[19]

Across from him on the grandstand to the right, looking like a sweet but scrawny go-along-to-get-along nonentity ripened in the sun of bourgeois prosperity, hung his younger brother, called "Cry-Baby." [20]

Both brothers hailed from Lübeck, the city where marzipan, that most delicate of all German confectionery, is manufactured. When they were born, instead of using pure linen, their mother swaddled them in best quality handmade paper (from fiction published by Semmi Fischer in Berlin and Kurt Wolff in Leipzig). The valiant father said: "If we can afford it, our talented sons should study to become 'poets.'" The babies cooperated by promptly crapping lyrically into their diapers. Eventually, through long and arduous effort, they both became true German cultural Delphic oracles.

Everybody who was anybody in the realm of national culture sat at the feet of these two oracular personages. One represented a round convex, the other a narrow concave reflection, each the counter-image of the other. On the right, Tomi stood for the classical stylist, on the left Heini represented romantics and radicals.[21]

"What twits!" thought Boche de Trocadero. "They provide the bourgeoisie with a pleasant way to pass the time in leisure and boredom. They run assiduously after trends and believe themselves to be the pole stars of eternity. If a Bonaparte appears they rattle their sabers, all war-like, But if a Gregor appears they cast their eyes piously to heaven.[22] And they call that evolution! They are plaster, stucco, façade, gilt ornamentation on the building of history. Only power rules supreme, and I am that power. I, Boche the Iron Marshal!"

Boche feared only *one* man in the room. Better said (because a Boche de Trocadero fears neither hell nor devil), he found him creepy.

He was a small, thin, bald-headed gentleman with a harmless-looking face sitting in the furthest corner of the room, biting off clipped words and numbers into a telephone receiver.

This enigmatic personage was Herr Mannheimer, proprietor of Mandelsüß & Co., the great national banking firm. Nobody had ever fathomed his thought processes. He sat in the corner like a Norn, weaver of destinies, holding the threads of fate in his hands. By approving or denying credit, he could influence republics and monarchies, cause war and revolution. Although nothing escaped his sharp eye and ear, he sat as though he had nothing to do with the proceedings, indifferent to fame and fortune of those sitting on high or below. In fact, he couldn't have cared less about any of them! He sat calmly, spewing numbers into his telephone, using a confidential system known only to him and his ever-attentive confidants, turning letters and numbers into syllables and sentences. An army of subordinate banks bought or sold securities according to Mannheimer's instructions. His computer-like mind calculated debits and credits from every twist and turn in world history, and everything that befell mankind—good and bad—served only as grist to the mill of his world-overpowering profiteering.

Marshal Boche was secretly terrified by this man, sitting in a corner with an unlit cigar in his mouth spitting words into a telephone. Here his world-conquering power ended. He saw before him, in the guise of that insignificant looking Mannheimer, a *satanic mind*, arranging revolutions or wars by telephone, bending the world's fate to his will through mystical logic. It seemed appropriate for the *Herr Reichspräsident* to say a few well-chosen words at the Marshal's Grand Opening ceremony.

Guschen Ehrlich was an oh-so-well-behaved man, but he wasn't the brightest bulb on the porch.

When his party came to power as a result of the Great Revolution following the lost war, it became clear that it didn't possess the necessary attributes to run a country. The giant bureaucratic pyramid glorying under the name "The State" was governed by a peculiar law, whereby intellect increases or decreases in inverse proportion to body weight, depending on position on the apex or base of the pyramid.

Said another way: larger brains that weigh a great deal tend to drag their owners down like lead, but lighter brains float up to the surface like cork. In this way, the upper levels of the pyramid's bureaucracy are most appropriately occupied by "massive bodies with relatively little intellectual capacity."

This law (the so-called Mach-Einstein axiom)[23] establishes the authority, even necessity, of monarchical form of government. Only by a long incestuous process can the noblest lineages in the land be carefully bred to take their place as the predetermined leaders in a God-given monarchy.

This axiom greatly embarrassed the party which gained power through revolution, because they had no suitable monarchical replacement. All party members had been made too "intellectual" by their nation's suffering, which also had the effect of arousing their spirit.

A suitably respectable candidate for Reich President, above suspicion and acceptable to all fellow Germans,[24] was required. It was decided to leave deliberation of this existentially important matter to the party members of Elias Müller, an established experimental psychologist from the Göttingen school.[25]

In Guschen Ehrlich, Müller found the most suitable candidate for the position of Reich President, according to the Mach-Einstein suitability quotient (i=0/d.∞) "After all, he is almost a Hohenzollern," Müller said, and Ehrlich was elected unhesitatingly to the highest office in the land.

Because Ehrlich was a good-hearted man who wore his arm on his sleeve and was easily moved to tears, he began his weighty address to the people with the suitable words: "During these difficult days" and ended with "Think, honored sirs, that we bear the historical responsibility for as yet unborn German generations." No politician or minister paid the slightest attention to anything he said or heard him out to the end. But it was obvious that this was the right note to pluck on the people's heartstrings. Someone *had to* take the role of his starving, tortured people's tragic muse, and no one fitted the bill as well as Ehrlich.

The Reich President's words rose into the air like a blue balloon[26] filled with fresh hydrogen. While he droned "In these difficult days," Tünnes the Younger, nature's blond favorite, turned to Foreign Minister Emil Blender,[27] requesting a brief tête-à-tête.

The meeting took place in a small side room of the People's House.

"Please sit down, Herr Doktor," the foreign minister said. He was a pleasant, jovial man. The bottom half of his face resembled a calm pasture of humanity, but the upper part was a craggy mountain of shrewdness.

"Dear Blender," Tünnes began, "I have just come from a meeting of the proletariat in Dollarcamp. The behavior of the Communists was a slap in the face to all usages of the class struggle. Labor leader Liebrecht behaved with such exaggerated patriotism that I fear a proletarian trick. Think of the worst case scenario: What if the working masses, inflamed by our patriotism, really *follow through*? Our situation would become impossible."

The foreign minister smiled, and a soft sunrise rose over the pastureland of his half-faced humanity.

"My dear Tünnes," he said, "you may be a great industrialist, but you are no politician. Did you *notice* nothing? What you experienced with young Liebrecht is nothing but a put-up job. We ourselves have staged this comedy. We gathered all the workers in the country around the Great Hall of the People, so that they would wait there right through these negotiations. We sent two thousand pro-regime anarchists out among them as spies with orders to keep on singing "La Marseillaise." My dear Tünnes, you have no idea of the power of music over the human heart. We will create a patriotic psychosis and allow it to spread across the whole country, threaten the proletariat with a lock-out until the soldiers are completely terrified, and use this sword of Damocles to take the pressure off us as much as possible. Leave Liebrecht to his own devices. We'll keep him on a short leash. If his patriotism becomes a nuisance, we'll simply get rid of him: we'll let it be known that he betrayed the class struggle and allowed himself to be bought by the government."

Tünnes The Great was accustomed to wandering through rooms of the great and powerful, sniffing out political tips. But, for now, he stood quietly next to his son, irritated by the foreign minister's hypocritical craftiness and Mannheimer's mocking indifference. He considered both men to be mortal enemies of "healthy national politics." A man used to hiding his own feelings, he gave the impression of arguing with his son. He cursed Baldur up hill and down dale, making sure that the foreign minister heard every word:

"Every general strike represents a sin against the nation. Production of goods and services is a country's life force. Export routes, colonies, ships and railways are the nerves of our being. Industry is our heart's blood and bone of our bones. If we party instead of working, we cannot pay. If we cannot pay, we invite violent retribution. We must work, work, work! Twelve, twenty hours a day if necessary! Only work can save us!"

Foreign Minister Emil Blender acted as if he had heard nothing. He stood up, walked back to the speaker's platform, unfolded a pile of papers, and started to speak.

After Guschen Ehrlich's basso profundo rumbling, Blender's clear tenor voice sounded like a fine steel blade cutting through the air inviting a duel:

"Honored sirs, I come here to warn you. You all know the story of the Bartholomew's Night massacre.[28] *Our* nation could prepare such a night of terror for the foreign usurpers as well. Even the most powerful cannons are ineffective against one particular form of violence. I am talking about national despair! We can put up with fifty percent, but more than that changes us into helots,[29] and our *Volk* will not put up with the yolk of helotism. If they are driven to extremes, they will turn to the only weapon they have left: *a general strike!*"

When they heard these words, politicians and soldiers alike turned pale. Even the marshal nervously twirled his little black mustachio.

Only the French industrialists smiled. Their faces shamelessly reflected the thought: "Surely you wouldn't saw off the branch on which we *all* sit."

Then something amazing happened. The voice of little Mannheimer resounded from the farthest corner behind the telephone, grating like a knife scraped against stone: "We are not merchants!"

He sat down, biting off mystical words into the telephone again.

Even the industrialists turned pale.

The bankers whispered to one another: "Did you hear? He is trading in a bear market." "Nonsense," said another, "he is *creating* a bear market."

Grand Old Man Tünnes was now thoroughly afraid.

He and Faussecocheur had a preliminary conversation. They had toured the great battlefields together and afterwards, during an enjoyable little visit to Monte Carlo, drawn up the points on which negotiations between the two nations should be based. But Mannheimer's behavior upset the applecart.

"God-damned Jew," the old man whispered to his enemy partner-in-conspiracy. "First he plays the conservative, now he is ruining our business on the world market."

"My dear man," Fausseoccheur smiled amiably, "*you* were the victim here. He hates your German National cause."

"You err, my friend," Tünnes replied, "he aimed this coin at *you*. Large scale industry can do nothing without international capital."

"Yes, industry," Faussecocheur retorted. (Tünnes couldn't figure out whether this was meant seriously or ironically). "Industry is always national, but banking is impartial. We are all our country's cavaliers, its financial swordsmen.[30] The fatherland is our favorite soup tureen: in Paris we call it *la marmite*."[31]

A tumult developed in the hall, and groups of people schmoozed in the galleries and aside rooms. The proletariat's attitude towards the convention had become threatening. The marshal's praetorian guard, arranged in two rows and occupying the exits with fixed bayonets, reported that it was becoming difficult to keep the crowd at a safe distance.

Suddenly the sound of "La Marseillaise" roared like thunder from the heath 10 kilometers away. It blocked out the sounds in the hall and people inside were forced to listen to the far-off din. During the general, anxious silence something else *more* alarming happened. A window pane rattled and cracked, and a stone flung from afar fell at the marshal's feet. Inkwells and ashtrays flew into the air, and many a resplendent uniform was splattered with ink.

Outside voices rang, and roaring hurrahs resounded. The name of Liebrecht was heard in the land: "Hurrah for Liebrecht!"

The dignitaries of the nation, Guschen Ehrlich at their head, next to him Chancellor Kuno Reisser, Culture Minister Gustav Gabbler,[32] War Minister Fungus von Fungusbeard[33] and Foreign Minister Emil Blender stepped out onto the balcony.

The heather was black with people as far as the eye could see. Flags and posters with the words: "Down with the enemy! Hurrah for a general strike!"

When they saw the government representatives on the balcony, those closest began to sing, and singing spread to the back of the crowd. "Hurray for Liebrecht!" They cried. "Let Tünnes the Younger speak!" Young Baldur, like a victorious, joyful god, stepped forward:

"Brothers! Fellow Germans![34] Fellow countrymen! Even though surrounded by armed soldiers, let us not be rash in this world-historical decisive hour!" (The first cries of *Pfui* echoed) "Let us prove ourselves as men." (*Bravo*! From the voices below).

"Hurrah for communism!" resounded from the crowd.

A worker in a blue blouse stepped onto a barrel and began to speak to the dignitaries on the balcony. His words were unclear, and no one knew for certain whether he recommended national or international unity. But the gist of his talk was that Jens Liebrecht must participate in the deliberations as representative of the working class.

"Good," the dignitaries on the balcony called out, "send Liebrecht up."

Tünnes Junior, hand on heart, solemnly replied to the man in the blue blouse: "At this difficult time, I know no party.[35] We are all brothers. Send your elected representative to the anteroom so that he can tell me what the workers demand of our government."

The joyful cadences of "La Marseillaise" resounded all over Dollarcamp. Remarkably, even the soldiers of the guard joined in.

While the government was sounding the people out and patriots of all stripes communicated with one another, Marshal Boche had a secret discussion with Faussecocheur inside the hall.

The Talleyrand of our time bent his foxy pointed beard-face, gleefully whispering in the Marshal's ear:

"You must admit, Monsieur le Maréchal, that we have arranged things splendidly. Even the stone worked wonders. The entire plain, two miles wide, is swarming with people, surrounded with our cannons. We can scatter them whenever we wish. We have infiltrated their ranks with 2,000 snitches (in reality Socialists devoted to the military cause), tasked to continuously cry 'hurrah for a general strike!' We have requisitioned 500 million marks from the Reichsbank, to support local reformers. Several dozen hitherto unrecognized geniuses have languished until now in the Düsseldorf lunatic asylum: we have freed them. Five hundred million for propaganda to 'support improvement of the human race' is a pretty tidy sum: for that amount we can have any form of government we wish. We have hung the revolutionary sword of Damocles over the government, to blackmail them as we see fit."

The marshal's limited military intellect finally grasped the trump suit that his politicians had dealt him.

Danger of a coup, double government, pitting the toiling masses against national defense, weakening the nation's élan vital, maybe even fomenting civil war. Revolution, whereby the illegal enemy invader sets forth the noblest motives to describe invasion as a blessing to civilization.

Marshall Boche began to see himself as the Savior of Europe, surrounded by pyrotechnic illumination.

But he was curious about the appearance of the Communist delegates. It was clear from the outset that the proletarian class must be set against German Nationalists. Boche had the warmest feelings for that genius of diplomacy whose machinations gave him control of Germany.

Jens Liebrecht stood waiting in the foyer between the sandstone pillars. His serious face was frazzled by efforts on behalf of the workers. He was a gentle and slender soul and still looked very young, although prematurely aged by early suffering. His clothes were clean but shabby and impoverished. He looked like a refined man whom the winds of fate had blown down deep into the proletarian pit.

He turned unceremoniously to Tünnes the Younger, as if they were two fellow-conspirators notifying each other of their plan, and whispered in his ear:

"Everything is prepared. The blast furnaces will be filled with earth. The dams on the Ruhr will be torn down and water will flood into the tunnels, rendering the river unnavigable. The workforce will melt away. If you bring in foreign labor, we will sabotage it. We will be poor, but free!"

Baldur looked stunned, and stammered: "What's all this? What do you really want?"

Liebrecht whispered: "Listen to me! Our national debt is 15 billion marks. That is the exact amount of your father's fortune. Together, we can save the fatherland. If you sacrifice your assets, the people will persevere, even if it takes years."

A sudden, terrible recognition coursed through the great French military scions. Was this man a fanatic? A lunatic? No! He was a master calculator. Or rather a catspaw of master calculators, shrewder than all assembled politicians combined. And he, Baldur Tünnes, soul of the fatherland's wealth—my God, what had he done? He had embraced this fellow and called him brother in full view of hundreds of thousands of workers!

They had known exactly how to compromise him by sending a representative who, on the surface, betrayed the international workers party to the fatherland, but in reality delivered the fatherland to the party bound hand and foot.

Deeply revolted, the words bubbled out of Baldur: "You really are all cold calculators! You have made us defenseless if we revolt at the enemy's armed intrusion. How wonderful! How much did the marshal pay you?"

Liebrecht tugged at his shabby jacket. He didn't seem in the least insulted.

"I've heard tell that our women have bound the men in corrals with their golden braids, so that none of them can sneak away. If they cannot triumph together they wish to die together."

"Stop it!" cried Tünnes impatiently. "At the very least you should have understood in your party schools that every country is connected to the world economy and cannot operate alone. Propagandistic rhetoric cannot make practical politics. Think about it! Let us assume that we deprive the enemy of our achievements by self-destruction. Would we be seen as national heroes? No! We would become Europe's gravediggers. If our nationalists are not prudent, patriots of foreign countries will bring us to our senses. They will have little or no understanding for an act of national self-destruction. To be a patriot for just a day means not to be a patriot at all, and not be a patriot for just a day is a demand for true patriotism."

Liebrecht took a step back, his face a mask of irrepressible pride. His icy cold words fell like an executioner's axe: "I see that you think like an internationalist, bound to old assumptions of the class struggle. Don't you understand? We cannot be ensnared in Marxist rhetoric or political economics at this difficult hour, when Germany's soul is on the line."

In country fairs, children young and old sit on fun ride wheels, for the peculiar enjoyment of being able to sway in all directions. Both

Liebrecht and Tünnes felt as if they were swaying on a rocker. They realized that each had become entangled in the other's catch-phrases. They were soldiers who had stolen each other's weapons. They stared inflexibly at each other. Tünnes the Younger was horrified: Liebrecht's eerie dark eyes seemed to penetrate his innermost soul. But, as the more socially adept, he had the strength to cut the knot.[36]

"Your Weltanschauung and conscience correspond: that is not our problem. We, that it to say all those who really feel strongly for *Volk* and Fatherland, are not prepared to sacrifice them on the altar of utopian experiments."

"Good!" the other said, "now I hear the way of speaking to which I have become accustomed. I can also be brief. I represent 300,000 workers waiting outside. We give you one hour to consider. If after this time you don't decide on a general strike, we will walk off the job on our own steam."

"That means a coup d'état."

"No, it means defense of the fatherland."

They measured each other up. Icy, cold, filled with contempt.

"Do you want civil war?" Tünnes panted.

"It is you who wants it."

"Can you guarantee one hour's calm?"

"The workers will maintain order."

"So wait for an hour. I will go and present your suggestions to the government."

"And I to my people. In an hour's time, we will enquire."

When Tünnes re-entered the Hall of the People under the Great Vault, he found the assembly dissolved into a hundred floundering, yelling, gesticulating groups of various sizes with no common, ascertainable purpose. What had happened?

The marshal wanted to send orders to his commissioned and non-commissioned officers to keep the peace, but it became obvious that telephone communications had been cut. He wanted to send orderlies out, but the workers surrounding the house declared that they would let nobody in and would not vacate the fields around Dollarcamp.

Both sides had taken the bit between their teeth. Both were boxed in. The people were surrounded by soldiers on two sides but, in their turn, they surrounded the Great Hall and it was impossible to get through the shoehorned throng of people without bloodshed. Communication with the nearest pickets, situated about an hour away, was impossible. If violence was used, the crowd would overrun the parliament in which Europe's greatest minds were gathered.

The parties in the hall fell over each other in mutual recriminations. All had played with fire and tried to make a nourishing broth out of the seething national soul. Now fire threatened to engulf them all. Faussecocheur, as representative of the occupation army, ascertained with the greatest outrage that an entire array of government snitches had been intercepted. They claimed to have been paid off by the local administration to foment a general strike. But an even greater sensation emerged, when the foreign minister calmly rose to announce that the *Herr* Faussecocheur was knocking on the wrong door. In reality, it was the occupation army who had paid no less than 5,000 snitches. Since 4.00 am that morning they had been trying to foment a general strike in the unhappy country. Even the guards surrounding the Great Hall had been poisoned by communism and were cooperating in an attempt to bring about a state of national confusion, to justify their illegal invasion by dressing it up as an attempt to restore political order.

Each side weaseled itself out of blame by trying to show that it had nothing to gain from a general strike. Only the Communist International and the rule of the mob would profit, gaining control of the poor country, followed by the whole of Europe.

It seemed as if the knotty problems of European politics had become insoluble.

Both sides had reversed roles. It was the old game of "musical chairs." The Nationalists dressed up as Communists, the Communists as patriots, the foreigners, who had incited the country to revolution in the first place, as guardians against revolution. No one saw clearly anymore. The only thing that both sides agreed on, in the guise of patriotism, was that this was a good time to exploit the collapse of the constitution.

But if the politicians didn't see clearly, the general staff certainly did.

Who dominated at that specific moment? Precisely those whom their opponents wanted to dominate, those at whose enslavement the invasion was directed: The workers, stuck between mortar batteries.

Luckily the dumb people didn't think or know anything! But did anyone really understand what was happening? We are not only speaking of the German government! No! The pole stars of the entire civilized world—those few thousand enlightened souls who represented the best the civilized world had to offer, held together on one little patch of ground like at no previous time in history.

Marshal Boche de Trocadero discussed the strategic situation with his adjutants and staff officers. Ten divisions were positioned around on the heights at a distance of four hours' travel. No one could reach, them. A thousand men stood guard round the house but, despite their weapons, they were not equipped to withstand a mass attack. If the commissioned or non-commissioned officers did not remain peacefully at arms or tried something on their own, catastrophe beckoned. If the troops advanced or opened fire, if there was even the appearance of hostility or possibility of danger, the consequences would be terrible. Because then the mass of 300,000 people assembled on the plain, already incited to revolution and work stoppage, would see no way out and storm the Great Hall of the People. They would cry havoc and unleash the dogs of war in an instant. For the masses, it would be simple—rather than subdue a government that lacked all authority—to crush representatives of the enemy country and take them captive. Properly led, the crowd could trap the famous personalities in the Great Hall and hold them hostage. They could negotiate independently with the soldiers and declare: "If you don't agree with our demands and take any hostile action, we will simply bump the hostages off."

Naturally, the people would have to believe this. If permitted, the soldiers would clean the place up, even kill all the people with massed fire. But would that be of any *use* to Europe's leading lights? They would all end up biting the dust.

"A very uncomfortable situation," remarked Marshal Boche de Trocadero.

"Your penetrating intelligence has hit the nail on the head again," replied Faussecocheur. "It is true that we are deeply in debt to each other. Each side has been caught in the other's trap. But I still have one hope: our army's cowardice."

The Marshal boiled over: "How dare you!" he raged. Cowardice? Soldiers who have the honor to serve under my command?"

"Mon cher Monsieur le Maréchal," said Faussecocheur, "Pray to the Lord of Hosts that our glorious army loses its nerve. It would save our necks if they all deserted. But think of the worst case: that all our countrymen are as heroic as you are! Or that their patriotism is as great as that of the local Communists. These people provoke each other with obscenities. They are packed too closely together in a rat trap, and tread one another's toes. Even the quietest and most devoted of men begins to be become enraged after a day without food or sleep. Cloudless skies, no rain, nothing to do for a day without end. Such things can make history. Imagine crowds of people loitering around for hours with nothing to do. They sing, drink, speechify, poison themselves with patriotism. Suddenly a shot is fired. That's enough—panic! The sheep push forward: they are still several hours from the Great Hall. There is only *one* solution. Communism! Luckily, our troops have been instructed to nurture Communist feelings. It's the new normal for our troops to keep singing 'La Marseillaise,' according to the order of the day. Soldiers aren't politicians. Please excuse me for saying this, but the national psyche is a very straightforward thing. Experience teaches us that apolitical people find it difficult to play a role without becoming the role that they play. If they sing patriotic songs for an hour, they feel patriotic. If they are permitted to sing Communist songs for an hour, they all become Communists. As for me, I wish that the entire world felt like Communists. Actually, a part of me really *doesn't* wish it. Because patriotic recklessness of Communist workers exceeds all bounds of justified national consciousness. Because this class of people are not brought up properly, they lack all concept of moderation. Instead of one orange, they buy twelve. Luckily, we have few patriots in our army. The best are from Morocco."[37]

While Marshal Boche and Faussecocheur were conferring, one satisfied individual ensconced himself in the corner. He was the only one who remained in the best of spirits during the course of that dangerous day. He was Mannheimer, proprietor of the great banking company Mandelsüß & Co.

Mannheimer didn't budge from his favorite spot. Because his telephone didn't work, he couldn't toss any more mystical signals into it. But that didn't seem to worry him in the least. He enjoyed one of the few leisure hours of a life in which every idle moment cost a billion marks. Although he still made calculations out of habit, his main preoccupation was, cold cigar in hand, muttering explanatory key words and phrases at the people around him. It wasn't clear whether he was making fun of them, or was serious about it. Both were possible. From time to time he came out with oracular pronouncements in his scratchy voice, of which the following is an example:

"Two things are necessary, but *one* is essential. First, genuine Christianity and brotherly love for all. Second, love for the fatherland and national honor. *Our* point of view combines both. The Christian-National Jesus—Christ, my hope and my salvation! O Fatherland, o glorious country, land of ancient loyalty!"[38]

"Stop it!" cried Tünnes the Elder, his archenemy. "You're making our politicians nervous!" Tünnes The Younger strode through the hall. Hardly had he mounted the speaker's platform, beckoning and flourishing his handkerchief, when the hall became quiet as a mouse.

The groups dissolved. In the passages, the side rooms, the stands—all tiptoed back to their seats, trembling with great but restrained excitement. Every cubic centimeter of the Great Hall was electric with tension.

Tünnes the Younger began with gasping breath: "The House is surrounded and the Communists are demanding a general strike. The guards seem to be fraternizing with the workers' leaders. We have been given one hour. If within that time a general strike is not approved, the Communist Party will take over the country's defense."

Wild outcries from the platform and in the hall.

"Oho! Listen! Listen!"

"*You* are responsible for this," local industrialists raged to the out-of-towners. But the latter yelled back: "quite obviously, it's *your* fault."

Tünnes the Younger waited until things had quietened down, and then said in a breathless, jumpy, clipped tone:

"Honored Sirs! I implore you. We are fellow passengers on a sinking ship, in battle against the forces of chaos. The decision before us is: Will order reign, or will the mob prevail? On which side will the government stand? What security can the marshal give us? We only have an hour to decide."

Before he could say anymore he was interrupted by a storm of protest.

Some yelled: "Unheard of!" Others: "Our patriots are acting like Bolshevists!" Yet others: "Our Communists are patriots!"

Everyone tried to out yell the other. Eventually the voice of Tünnes won out, and was heard again in the land:

"I hear the suit and the charges,[39] but we have no more time. I don't need to tell you that I am no Spartacist,[40] but I believed that the Communists loved their fatherland as well. I erred in greeting their leader as a brother today, and now they have saddled us with it. How could I have predicted that the Communists would abuse the situation to stoke up terror?"

The politicians laughed.

A buoyant baritone voice was heard from the parterre: "What a stunt! No-ne!"

It was the voice of the leader of the Democratic Party, the gracious Baron von Soonwillhave.[41]

He was the leader of a banking company, and had the lovable habit of speaking German with a Yiddish accent.[42]

"Laughable!" someone called out from the podium. Everyone was overjoyed to have found a scapegoat.

Foreign Minister Emil Blender immediately saw how he could use this as a safety valve to vent the general moral indignation.

"Well you see, *Herr Doktor* Tünnes," he said, "that's what happens when a party plays politics on its own without governments knowledge. Now the government must get out of the pickle that the German People's Party[43] has created."

"What a scene!" cried the gleeful baron.

Tünnes The Elder, who bullied his son at every opportunity but became really furious if anyone else tried to do the same thing, planted himself in front of his son. Despite seeing through the tactical error, he responded sharply: "No one can fault it when, at the fatherland's most difficult hour, two groups of fellow Germans[44] call each other brother. Our party believes in the patriotism of the *other*. We have both been deceived, and must now fight a battle on two fronts. We must make common cause and fight with the internal against the external, but also with the external against the internal enemy."

"Indeed," cried Faussecocheur, "we can solve the riddle right here. Where is the enemy?"

General embarrassment and confusion.

Marshal Boche restored order and quiet by loudly sounding the bell three times.

In the meanwhile, he discussed the matter with Faussecocheur.

"My dear marshal," Faussecocheur said, "by all means scare these idiots half to death but in heavens name don't create a crisis, Give these kaffirs[45] the feeling that danger lurks everywhere. At the same, time, give them the feeling that they and they alone can guarantee security no matter what danger threatens. The world always yields to security. If one has none, this is the way to act."

Calm was finally restored and the marshal could again make himself heard:

"Esteemed assembly! As a soldier, I must always deal with the possibility of death. But have no fear. Our loyal army is unshakably patriotic, and will protect this foreign land from revolution. Yes, we will protect you! We will administer European law and order! But, within the hour, we have to make a decision that calms the striking proletariat. Should the government endorse the general strike, or declare it invalid?

As far as *we*, representatives of the occupation army, are concerned, we can summarize our position as follows: If the government endorses the general strike, we will arrest them and take responsibility for law and order in your country ourselves. If the government doesn't endorse the general strike *we* will endorse it and let the excited masses go home with the message that the government has endorsed it. This measure may appear somewhat strange to you. But what else can we do to convince the people of a country that besieges us here to go home?"

Perplexity reached a fever pitch.

"Does anyone else wish to add anything?" asked Faussecocheur.

Guschen Ehrlich, as senior member of the government, felt obliged to say something. He pumped up his supply of hot air, stood up, and started to drone: "During these difficult days…" but those around him pushed him back onto his gilded throne, saying: "Banal words mean nothing, Excellency. These are serious political issues, and must be dealt with politically. Let Kuno Reisser or Emil Blender handle it."

The blue balloon collapsed into his chair, totally deflated. Slender and elegant, the picture of cold, detached masculinity, Emil Blender rose, removed the monocle from his right eye, blew a speck of dust from it, ceremoniously took a silk handkerchief from his waistcoat pocket, and began, holding the lorgnon gracefully between two fingers, carefully polishing its gleaming surface.

"Sirs," he began, "the political situation is crystal clear and corresponds with our wishes and expectations. If the majority doesn't wish to work with the enemy (as appears to be the case), we will support them. But please honored military and political experts, think seriously about the fact that, if *this* happens, we cannot guarantee your lives. As a member of the human race and a Christian, I wish with my whole heart that you all come out of this hall with your heads intact. However…I have complained about this before…the Great Hall of the People doesn't have enough toilets. The situation is atrocious—you all have the trots, and the toilets are all full. Well, my dear sirs, you will just have to sit awkwardly and accept some well-chosen truths. *I* don't have to express them in words. Vox populi, not so? Words from the outside speak to you more loudly than my own: 'You will never force us to work for your cash box by force! Never! A nation bound and intent on destroying its own manufacturing base rather than be forced to rejoice in the privilege of working for you, that desires no gain and cannot be *blackmailed*—eventually even you will have to understand this.' So, at the last minute, I have a suggestion, to save the day."

Blender re-inserted his monocle and paused portentously for several moments. Finally, he continued:

"The army of occupation is leaving the country and the population will soon receive official notification. With that, the reason for a general strike has disappeared, and the Communists have lost their raison d'être. As compensation, we offer one third, no, let's say 40%, of the national net income. Considering the changing conditions, that should be a tidy piece of business for you…"

Faussecocheur rose at once, to put his five cents in. He was amiable, unbiased, and even cooler and more detached than Blender.

"Esteemed guests," he began, "we are certainly on the horns of a dilemma, which doesn't entirely lack piquant originality."

He interrupted himself, seeming to notice something amiss with the gold lead holder with which he was doodling figures on a piece of paper while speaking. He fussily took a small case of graphite points out of his waistcoat pocket, replacing the one he had been using. He gave the impression that *this* was the center of his interest, and that he airily dismissed what he was saying as being of no importance whatsoever.

"Honored sirs, the current situation is indeed piquant—it resembles which of two merchants on a powder keg will be blown up first. You cannot be blamed for trying to exploit this opportunity as rapidly as possible for your own particular advantage. But you misjudge the parallelogram of forces.[46] The alternative—Spartacist or rescue of national industry—applies to you, not us. The question of chaos or currency stabilization applies to you, not us. We, on or side, cannot but sympathize with the gentlemen from the Communist World League who are of the opinion that the time has come to consummate the world revolution over which they have already spilled a sea of words. This even though, based on our more mature political experience, we cannot share the utopian optimism of the International Proletariat. We cannot withhold our sympathy for two reasons. Firstly, because, of all nations on earth, only yours and ours have consistently raised the standards of liberté, egalité, fraternité. Secondly, because, from the German National point of view, we consider the conduct of the Communist International no less understandable and moving than the concern of the bourgeois propertied class for preservation of their commercial assets and national industrial competitiveness. The foreign minister's suggestion, although delivered a little too heatedly to be politically debatable, shows us how seriously he *should* be taken, and distresses and astonishes us. It was never our purpose to concern your worthy government with drafting of positive recommendations. Our own tax commissions must alone decide which reparations or quotas must be paid, and we expect them to do their duty to the best of their abilities. But *another* question stands before us: does your government really *wish* to proclaim a general strike? Whether you wish so or not, I fear that our sincere and well-meaning offer to negotiate with you and your country's government will soon be withdrawn. We will have to wait and see whether the leader of the new government will refuse to cooperate with our non-political and unilaterally patriotic efforts to consolidate Europe."

Another wave of helpless embarrassment swept through the hall. Suddenly, Mannheimer's dulcet tones crackled from his corner: "*Mandelsüß & Co. will finance the general strike.*"

After all!

Iacta alea est!

The industrialists looked around speechlessly.

The bankers sat flabbergasted.

They all made a rough estimate of the national economy's shares and bonds. No question: all industrial instruments had taken a hit.

Grand Old Man Tünnes couldn't keep it in any longer:

"First Blender, now Mannheimer! So it's really true that our national banking business is *murdering* our fatherland's industry!"

As a German patriot, Tünnes had invested many billions in national shipyards, mine share certificates and secure branches of industry. He owned 148 daily newspapers of every political persuasion, 50 press and 20 telegraph agencies, 24 wireless telegraph stations, and 5 undersea cables.

He had transferred much of his capital *in good time*. But is it fair that the fatherland's industry must atone, if it doesn't move *all* its capital out of the country?

The grand old man jumped up: an exasperated black jaguar:

"Sirs! Men in whose blood love for the fatherland flows!" (Bravo! From the platform)—"those without love of country can easily pantomime true patriotism. Love of fatherland is, for international communism, only a matter of speculation. We, by contrast, bear the entire weight of the nation's business on our shoulders. For us, world economic solidarity is a matter of practical experience, and representation of the national interest is something concrete and tangible. On one side stands the reckless spirit of destruction, on the other the healthy organic evolution of Europe. On closer examination, it has become very clear to me that the Freemasons and Jews are at least partially to blame for the parlous situation in which we find ourselves."

"Don't forget the bicycle riders," called Mannheimer from his corner.

"Why the bicycle riders?" asked a perplexed Tünnes

"Why the Jews?" replied Mannheimer.

Baron von Soonwillhave's cheerful baritone echoed from the parterre:

"Well? So what?"

"Adjourn!" the dignitaries on the platform cried.

"Order! Order!" boomed Guschen Ehrlich's beery baritone like an avenging God hovering over the proceedings.

Order broke down completely.

In vain did Marshal Boche threaten to send thirty uniformed police to the hall of mirrors and punch every intellectual in the gut, kick him in the shins, even fire at him, if he interfered with the proceedings. But the luminaries in the hall of mirrors had understood one salient fact: they could not be *thrown out.*

All of them were convinced that they had *solved* the so-called culture problem.[47] Their lives revolved around linguistic interplay that they had ingested with mother's milk. For example: mechanical and organic, state and people,[48] international and national, and similar pleasant dialectic exercises.

Everyone made a hobby out of noble comical word synthesis, and couldn't wait to be the first to show his contemporaries how to save the world. Young men full of cosmogenic hope and orphic style virgins from "Mr. Shakespeare's circle" had long since agreed to give Cry-Baby a hearing at the nation's fateful hour.

Tomi was not one to shirk his national responsibility. Because he was exempted from front line duty for medical reasons, he had contributed to the war effort by helping to set up a charity bazaar, with a picture of his villa in Berchtesgaden, decorated with his signature: "May the war last for seven years, to uphold the glory of the German heroic spirit."[49]

Tomi had worked his whole life to project a "good guy image." For that reason, he at first modestly refused to place himself in the limelight. Later however, on general request, he changed his mind.

The pillars of artistic creation raised him on their shoulders, and the Nereids and Tritons of poetry tooted on their pocket combs, house keys, and cigarette butts. They rose into the arena and placed him on the podium.

There he stood. A velvet stool was shoved under his feet, to accentuate his "good guy" image. He took a sip of raspberry lemonade and took his manuscript out of the pocket of his tuxedo.

The silence was tangible. National self-esteem and cultural worth dictated that, in this fateful hour, a national oracle would emerge out of the whirlpool.

Tomi read out:

"Conscience, a deeply ingrained moral-artistic character trait has, times without number, constrained my lonely voice crying in the wilderness. I have taken it upon myself, alone and unaided, to ensure the literary, psychologic, and artistic strength of our proud nation with all the loyal power that I, humble servant that I am, have at my disposal. I have tried my best to distance my own ego in favor of the fatherland's political interests. Because what is art, if not ethics personified? I am no giant monocled Junker with a coarse and brutal laugh. I live in a world of civilized behavior. Mine is a world of urban elegance and solidarity, of *Kultur* not internationalism like the elegant bourgeoisie. My instinctual aspiration for dignity and comfortable material opulence is based upon ancient values and differs from the prodigality of the national bourgeoisie.

"Political actions carried out by the barrel of a gun can only be authorized and justified if they can be protected from the barrel of a gun.

"Am I sure of this?

"I have many faults, amongst these a perhaps unmanly willingness to adopt and affirm spiteful character stylization. But I am a *poet*, and we poets are all pushovers for a sense of validity. Deep, moving, crafty, perfidious, full of feeling, devious, somewhat cowardly, a little wishful and envious of healthy, Aryan life that is too brutal to fully understand our manifold sensitivities; dubious, but full of attention for essence and existence,[50] even for my dog, a tram conductor, my maidservant.

"Observe the oyster, honored Sirs, with its beautiful mother of pearl shell. What lies inside? A small, slimy, boneless, unbeautiful piece of jelly. It has no skeleton; therefore it builds one in the form of a pearl. Observe the lantern-carrying world-illuminating lightning bug: Professor Freud[51] has taught us that its glow really represents sublimation of the sexual instinct. In essence, it is only a dirty, little worm, like a poet in the world of his *achievements*. The all-civilizing literary figure differs: he is political, personal, allocutory, radical, humanistic, and—in a disgusting sense—*noble!*"

The nobility of Europe (politicians, soldiers, industrialists, bankers) looked around astonished.

They took away only two things from this verbal diatribe: a poet must be a *special* type of person, and a dark sense of their own inferiority.

But delegates in the hall of mirrors understood Tomi's gentle malice only too well. The Phrygian ladies[52] from the circle around Männe

Senior had their long sharp hatpins at the ready, and yelled angrily that Männe Shakespeare must immediately prepare to defend himself.[53]

Tomi ploughed on to the end regardless: "We are talking about the differences between the masses and a people[54] between individual and personality, civilization and *Kultur*, social and metaphysical life. Communism is the spirit of society, but that spirit is hate! By contrast, the soul is love![55] The fatherland is the soul of community."

Hardly had he finished speaking when, to parliament's amazement, an opponent blared out the following words:

"This is all rubbish! The exact opposite is true! Nationalism is the soul of society and communism is the spirit of the community!"[56]

All hell broke loose.

A replacement of principles was demanded.

Groups formed all over the hall.

Dialectic, phenomenologic, socialist, expressionist, anthroposophic, neoreligious. A beginning was made to "solve all the problems and conflicts of modern culture."

Surrounded by a crowd of worshipful noble ladies, Count Klingaling, Germany's philosophical Ganges farmer, the Darmstadt self-seeker, held court.[57] He demonstrated with Kantian clarity that the "national versus international" antithesis underlying all dissensions boils down to a polar split in world unity. This polarity is a conscious but timeless observational fact, which *may* be overcome by "cosmic vision" and *could be* harmonized by all possible points of view.

At the opposite end stood the concept-libertine Splintshaver the Schnitzelmaker[58]—heir to the great Hegel[59]—who challenged Klingaling's narrative. It was "fictitious" and should be replaced by Goethe's botanical writings on the clonal morphology of twenty-eight cultured souls.[60] Although one of these clones—European development—had arrived at the final stages of its cultural demise, this was no reason for "wimpy pessimism," but rather a world of "healthy, life-affirming go-getters" exemplified by Cecil Rhodes,[61] Grand Old Man Tünnes, and a third whom modesty prevented him from naming.

In the meanwhile, more than three quarters of an hour had passed.

Ten minutes remained, but no information could yet be given to those waiting outside, so they whiled the time away reading *Kladderadatsch*.[62]

Tünnes the Younger and the Elder, Marshal Boche, Guschen, Emil Blender—all were honestly willing to restore order. But nothing seemed to work.

The intellectuals raged unrelentingly.

Eventually Faussecocheur hit on the only solution. He called for the large fire hose attached to the water pipe crane to be carried into the Great Hall and sprayed mercilessly onto the intellectuals.

That finally did the trick.

From the platforms: "Stop it! Stop spraying us!"

In the ensuing silence a cry was heard from fat Thiessen, a.k.a. Cannon Thiessen. It struck the landscape, under threat of death, like a lightning bolt: *profit-sharing*.

All practical politicians looked at each other. It was a God-given natural revelation, indicating a way out of their impasse.

Faussecocheur rose, saying: "We ask Herr Thiessen for positive suggestions."

Thiessen responded:

One-third *Akaaaavau* (*Allgemeiner kommunistisch-anarchistisch-antinational-apolitischer Arbeiter-Verband* [General communist-anarchistic-antinational-apolitical worker's union].

One-third *Örka* (*Occupations-Eintreibungs-Requisitions-Ausschuß*) [Occupation-levy-requisition-committee)

One-third *Avikage* (*Allgemeine vaterländisch internationale Kanonen-Aktiengesellschaft*) [General patriotic international cannon corporation].

A thoughtful silence ensued. Eventually Kuno Reisser came forward and filed a motion to vote for work leader Liebrecht to serve on the *Avikage* supervisory committee.

The Grand Old Man bent over and whispered into the ear of his co-expert archenemy: "He'll soon realize that utopia cannot heal humanity."

"Quite right, my dear colleague," Faussecocheur smiled jovially, "but it is *we* who will direct the business."

"We request the appearance of Herr Liebrecht," Marshal Boche said. "Parliament wishes to hear him."

An inhabitant of a peaceful Australian South Sea island abducted by air ship from his Gauguinian palm-fronded idyll to Broadway, New York City would have had the same feeling as Liebrecht, suddenly placed before the rulers of the earth in the Great Hall of the People.

Dignitaries awaited him at the door. When he entered the hall, everyone jumped to their feet and stood on tiptoe. Everyone wanted to see him. Like a mooncalf who had just fallen off the moon, he ascended the speaker's podium.

Guschen Ehrlich started to blather again: "During these difficult days..." But Tünnes the Elder rudely and abruptly shut him up. "Sit down, *Herr* Reich President!"

"Liebrecht," he said, "it has fallen to you to save our fatherland. I knew your father, a loyal comrade in one of the mines. Save our country from useless bloodshed, and don't cooperate with the enemy. We implore you! Refusal to work would mean destruction of our national industry, national bankruptcy, suicide. Save our beloved country!"

Faussecocheur continued, with feigned indignation:

"Monsieur Liebrecht," he cried, "before you give an appropriate answer, be so kind as to allow me—although I represent a power repugnant to you—to properly repudiate this kind of horse-trading. If you haven't learnt it already in your own country, experience it from the mouth of a free spirit of a foreign nation for the first time. Communists have a fatherland, honor, and ideals as well! Our Honored and Revered Marshal Boche de Trocadero, Conqueror of Fatinitza, knows how to protect Communists in a foreign nation from the filth with which they are pelted, just because they are high-minded patriots. We don't want a revolution. Our goal is rather European harmony. But we are convinced that the *Herren* Liebrecht and Boche, who will from now on be negotiating *together*, will be guided by the ideals of liberté, egalité, and fraternité."

How did Jens Liebrecht, the Communist agitator, proceed?

He stood on the platform like on a rock in a burning ocean, hearing nothing, lost to the world, fists clenched, face twisted into a grimace, slumped over, incapable of understanding anything.

Suddenly, like a cataleptic turned uncontrollably raving mad and filled with wild loathing, he hurled one word into the hall: "*bastards!*"

He repeated the word, more softly, as justifying it to himself: "Yes, they *are* bastards!"

The effect was indescribable, exceeding even that of the sudden torrent from the rubber hose.

At first, the august assembly sat rigid with astonishment. Then fists were brandished. The cry came from many voices: "Throw him out! Impudent proletarian! Boor!"

But then they had second thoughts, and realized that they had no real power.

This young lout was sent to represent 300,000 men besieging the Great Hall of the People. Whenever they wished, they could sweep away the entire assemblage of Europe's noblest minds. This bumpkin was the only one who could prevent their collapse.

In the midst of general confusion, the sound of Mannheimer's voice was again heard in the land. He hopped with demonic joy from one leg to the other, crying: "Bravo! I agree completely with Herr Liebrecht!"

Faussecocheur, Boche, Blender and Tünnes the Elder all looked at each other. The penny finally dropped. They began to understood what was happening in its proper context.

Mannheimer and this proletarian ruffian were in cahoots. They were untouchable, despite the most shameless abuse of their power.

"You have before you, dear Faussecocheur," said Boche (his eyes shrouded in melancholy), "proof of how destructive it is when an ordinary man becomes an autocrat. You and I represent the principle of law and order. But when those two wretched creations, international financiers and the international mob, join together, what *remains* of human ideals? The course of world history is terrible. It drives one to lose all faith in God."

Jens Liebrecht on the speaker's platform was the picture of misery.

Before him he saw a sea of angry faces—from each, telescope-like, a pair of resentful, malevolent eyes stared. A vague cloud of steam and dust hovered over them all, illuminated by a yellow light.

The day waned. In the late afternoon, the gallery pillars cast bluish shadows. A waterfall-like rumbling was heard from afar, the sound of workers gathered around Dollarcamp. Everything was covered with impenetrable thick fog. Liebrecht didn't see, or think clearly about, what had happened.

Fragments of images danced around in his head. His entire life suddenly flashed before him like a drowning man, tied up in a confused knot, a dream-like thicket which no ray of light could illuminate.

He saw his red brick house, behind it the sparse kitchen garden with two apple trees. Clear as day, he saw the hawthorn hedge around the property in which wild roses straggled. A lime pit lay behind the garden. Next to it piles of yellowish sand from which children built castles. Then came potato and turnip fields from which boys made stubble fires. It was fall: kites rose in the wind.

Two days ago, Spahis[63] had marched in and set his youthful paradise ablaze.

He saw the picture of a young woman, the hectic flush of consumption on her too-early faded face: his mother, who had died too young. Then his father: bent over, shriveled up, crushed by hard work.

Picture after picture of coal mines, deep underground, rose up before him,

Metallic tunnels cut through the barren rock. Deposits and seams of coal and ore creep forward: the powerful dragons of prehistory lurking in the mountains. Greedy serpents hunt them down: trial tunnels and shafts. With hammers and bars, tools of their trade, in their hands men crawl ant-like through the passageways. Their faces are ashen and pale. Eyes half blind. The air in the mine, a deadly threat lurking in the depths. Mine carts and hand carts rattle from gallery to gallery. Horrible coal-black lakes, the eyes of hell, cast reflected shine on the rocky walls. Though miles away, the good and faithful lung keeps pumping: the ventilation fan does its work. The miner's headlamps flit about. Fireflies among the leaves. They offer some comfort to the tortured animals, the exhausted men.

Liebrecht saw factories, machine shops, steel rolling mills, smelters, chimneys, smokestacks.

Levers, cranks, bullock gears, winches, hoists, wheels and axles, rotors, treadmills.

Tender children, weakly women, exhausted old men.

Throng after throng, generation after generation. Abused, exploited, blocked from all sun and starlight, made into nothing but screws and wheels, numbered and interchangeable.

In looms, skimmers, shearing, engraving, glazing, and machine tool machines.

Of course! They didn't even need to starve and freeze. They had all the animal delights imaginable, as compensation during long hours of free time. They had bars and cinemas, after all. Civilization's profiteers, spare employees. Penitents in jail cells, she-wolves on sidewalks, rags in the gutter, miserable wretches. They were *all* betrayed. For the sake of beauty and soul!

The great lie of all-powerful exploiters buzzed in his brain: "You only work for 8 hours, then you are free. We, however, we are the ones who think, calculate, organize, combine. We work without stopping, much harder than you do—24 hours a day! What do *you* do compared to our noble efforts?

Of course! In conferences such as these, leaning comfortably in leather chairs, smoking cigars. In the great banking and stock exchange halls. in the spas, hotels, parliamentary halls, dining rooms of luxury ships and trains. After all, trade and reasoning must be combined with the finer things in life, but not too much physical exertion, if you please! World history created between drinks…Who called you to squander the world away for the sake of pleasure?

Confused intuitions swirled through his mind that there wasn't a single man in this assembly who could understand a word he said.

His mind was a jumble of rhetorical exercises from his party school—dialectical phrases of European Communist theory. An endless caravan of hopeless, helpless souls, objectified, exploited, dehumanized, used as a means to an end, passed before his lonely eyes.

A wilderness of dreams, untouched by light, swirling around in his head.

They had voted *him* as their mouthpiece, the voice of their pain. But he was inexperienced in the ways of the world, awkward, lacking original ideas.

He had always been condemned to stand alone in a corner: forced back, alienated, passed over, until he became hostile to the entire "human race."

Nothing was clear to him, he believed in nothing. Everything was "so different."

He wanted to serve his fatherland. But by doing so, wouldn't he destroy the soul of his party? And *if* he served his party, wouldn't he set his face against his country's welfare?

He felt as if all the sluices of his soul had been opened at the same time. All the torments of his lonely existence, dammed up for so long, now gushed forth together. Condemned to perpetual silence, destiny had given him the opportunity to speak, bleed out, and thereby fulfil himself.

Jens Liebrecht spoke:

"You sit here preening in the Great Hall, bargaining with people's sweat and blood. When it suits you, you cry: 'Rise up, my children! Die a hero's death! The fatherland is in danger!'

"What *is* the 'fatherland'? Your castles and villas filled with priceless tapestries and paintings? Your interest, rents, vouchers, dividends —that the poor workhorse, fenced in by hallowed tradition, has pulled out of the fire for you, as he always does?

"August 1914.

"Do you remember the slogan then?

"Our poor homeland, shining star of discipline, heart of the earth, morality's pledge—our sacred homeland, surrounded by enemies, envied, gagged by all.

"What did you want then? To enrich yourselves, make a killing, annex more land, expand your power!

"What did Europe look like? Five dogs chained next to one another. Each greedy, mistrustful, envious, uneasy one with the other. If a bone is thrown to them, they go for each other's throats and tear each other to pieces.

"Good! That might be world history, but did that serve our upsurge in patriotism, our vows? Did we die a hero's death for *that*?

"And now? It's as if fate has tested our souls' authenticity!

"All their lies *really* have come to pass. Now, at this exact moment, it makes all the sense in the world to demand: freedom or death!

"Why don't we make the ultimate sacrifice, and face death willingly? You say that it would be 'unpolitical,' achieving nothing. Does profit alone sanctify war, justify success, condemn injustice? I would prefer that we lock ourselves in the sacred sanctity of our nation and immolate ourselves, rather than lose our souls. But your blood is cold, your hearts dumb. So *we* will be the fatherland's outcast but only faithful son, and save our homeland."

Unbelievable rejoicing broke out all over the hall: politicians, industrialists, even representatives of the occupying powers were *spellbound* by his words. Thunderous applause echoed. Ladies waved perfumed handkerchiefs from the balcony. Journalists rushed to the window crying: "Liebrecht has spoken! Liebrecht is organizing our national defense!"

The working masses outside continued the cry: "Hurrah for Liebrecht!" alternately singing "La Marseillaise" and "Deutschland Über Alles."

Europe's greatest intellects sat around in the bottomless pit of the Great Hall like a mass of grinders, whose giant wheels were capable of turning even the heaviest boulders or granite blocks into *sand*.

Mental processing began at once.

Mirrors reflected, tongues wagged, brains evaluated, *Kultur* judged. They were ready to turn this "experience" into literature, and reduce it to historical proportions, in the good old-fashioned way.

In the old Imperial box. Countess Perponcher said to *Geheimrätin* Prinzheimer: "My dear Prinzheimer, this young worker cuts quite a dash: he must be from a better family." Prinzheimer, putting her red-dyed hair in order, answered graciously: "I will introduce him to you by inviting him to my *jours!*"

In the celebrity hall of mirrors, the board of the writer's association "Pointe" requested that Manny Shakespeare prepare a "formula for contemporary history."

His insightful formula was as follows:

"The young man is sincere, but not too intelligent. He did indeed spout an incompletely digested piece of Rousseau, but his own personal touch was unmistakable."[64]

After hearing this perceptive verdict, Cry-Baby's noble judgment was as follows: "Because the unsophisticated man cannot completely shed the highly reactive atmospheric gases of his environment, he cannot achieve the representative validity so evident to *all*. Politics is an objective art. To be an artist requires training. *Mine* is, above all else, the soul of a soldier. Therefore, I always guard against making my work for European validity too unenjoyable through dubious private character."

Thus spoke Cry-Baby (it was so very literary: he strode confidently where no man went. When others washed their faces, *he* bathed his countenance).[65]

Liebrecht's speech led to the most agreeable mood of general good will, promising to deal with all issues, even the thorniest, in the most impartial, honest manner possible.

The young man was somewhat green and brutally immature, but he had talent on which something good and important could be built. Perhaps a stock corporation, a periodical, a publishing house, a new cultural "direction." Certainly it wasn't nice that he had said "bastards," but blame is always shifted onto others, and everyone is happy when the slate is wiped clean by someone else.

Count Klingaling, Germany's self-seeker who lived joyfully near to God in Darmstadt's holy precincts, opined that "the naïve speech of this man of the people has finally raised negotiations to a high cultural niveau." By contrast, the more strong-willed Prussian-social Splintshaver the Schnitzelmaker held out against calling the workers too "literate"; they were not strong enough to be go-getters. Both key opinion leaders directed the orchestras of their ever-opposing "life views." There were reasons for this. Klingaling, like Peer Gynt, was always "himself" but *lent an ear* to the entire world. Splintshaver, like Wilhelm II, didn't listen to anyone but traveled all over the world, constantly talking whether anyone was listening or not.[66]

But everyone was sure that the Communist possessed the power (proven by his salutation "bastards"), and that his influence had to be reckoned with (in order to use him as a battering ram against the other parties). Everyone can be used, isn't that so?

Liebrecht's maiden speech had a curious effect on our national industry.

Behind the Reich President (whose purse of golden words had long since been spent) sat Coalkrupp, Tünnes, and Cannon Thiessen.

They looked into each other's faithful, blue German eyes and shook each other's noble, patriotic hand.

They understood each other. There was no more integrity, no more loyalty in this world. They were witness to history's most diabolical trick. The proletariat had succeeded in an opening act portraying itself as the larva and mask of their own honest faces.

"Truly, dear Tünnes," Cannon Thiessen said, "If the man had a cleaner collar, with an Iron Cross First Class on his chest, I would almost believe that I saw you *yourself* in younger days."

"God yes, Thiessen," said the Grand Old Man, "what a wonderful pair of Communists we've become. You know what we could *do*, if only we were *allowed* to do so. The preposterous thing is, that the Communists play the patriot, because they have no clue of the torments that we suffer curbing *our own* patriotism. Believe me, Thiessen, if I could, I would strangle that pig Faussecocheur with my own hands. What does love of fatherland demand of me? That I offer him my own cigars. That I entertain him with information about different brands of cognac. That I call him *Herr Kollege* while he is betraying me."

"If I only knew," Coalkrupp said thoughtfully, "whether that fellow really believes the poem that he recites to us."

Tünnes the Elder, that canny connoisseur of human nature, chimed in: "I consider the young man to be completely harmless. You see, my dear Coalkrupp, when one has spent as much time on politics as Thiessen and myself, the difference between what one says and what one believes (or doesn't believe) becomes blurred. Illiterate people corrupt healthy politics because they always believe what they say, and say what they believe. That is terribly dangerous!"

"I believe that, as erudite men, we must differentiate more subtly, my dear Tünnes," Thiessen whispered back. "A man expresses—and is believed to *have*—only one opinion. But does he *really* have only one?"

Our pure hearted local kings of industry would have wanted to execute their arch-enemy much less bloodily had they known the effect of Liebrecht's patriotic Communist speech on Boche and Faussecocheur.

"What impressed me the most," said Boche "was his *salutation*." It's peculiar that he rightly called both of us 'bastards.' For this reason, I fear that *he* is one as well."

Faussecocheur responded:

"I still see some rays of hope. I believe that he is an honest patriot, and is therefore up for grabs. I also believe that his feelings need to be diverted, by counteracting each of his ideals with a different one. What is the purpose of culture if not this? Even religion requires justification. There is something glorious about suggestion. During times of hunger the entire nation becomes a communal glutton. Why? Because attention is concentrated on one and only one thing: how can I eat my fill? As a result, they eat more than ever. Things are always what we think them to be. Concepts are power. I am an idealist, and believe in the power of ideas. I will approach Monsignore Nitti, the Apostolic Nuncio."

While Faussecocheur betook himself to Monsignor Nitti,[67] the national cabinet, headed by Guschen Ehrlich, gathered together in a side room, to set down the guidelines to which the Communists should adhere.

No one saw through the Communists' ulterior motives better than Emil Blender. He understood why Liebrecht's speech was purposely so dark and flowery at the same time. He also admired the provocative use of "bastards." Because he was a man who saw and understood everything in the world through "political" lenses, he glossed over the prospect of a coup d'état on both sides.

He never for a moment entertained the thought that this daring player would give vent to the ridiculous feelings in his ridiculous innermost heart. No! He, Emil Blender, was the shrewdest of the shrewd. He knew world history better than anybody!

Guschen Ehrlich was of an entirely different opinion. "Sirs," he said, "the esteemed Communists have, *despite all*, taken our propaganda in support of a general strike seriously, and the people's patriotic enthusiasm is thwarting our Erfurt program."[68]

"Excellency," Chancellor Kuno responded, "You misunderstand the nuances of European politics. The Communists have figured out that we cannot do what we pretend to want to do. Now they want to force us to *really* want what we previously wanted only for political reasons. They pretend to believe that we honestly want it and thereby force us to *really* want to do what we are not honestly *able* to want."

"That's a dirty trick!" said Guschen.

Culture Minister Sepp Schmoozer[69] added the following words of wisdom:

"It's a well-known fact that someone who wants to deceive never notices when they are deceived. Do you know the story of the two Polish Jews who were so used to telling lies, that they most easily deceived each other when they told the truth? Once they met at the Warsaw railway station: 'Where are you going?' the one rival asked the other. 'To Cracow' he replied. The other thought: 'Now you are trying to let me in on a lie. You are *not* traveling to Cracow; *I* am going there.' Afterwards they met in the same Cracow-bound train. The deceived Jew indignantly shouted: 'You *really are* travelling to Cracow. Why did you *lie*?'"

"This is, more or less, the Communist International's relationship with honest patriots like ourselves. Understandably, the Communists are using the moment when patriots are unarmed to outyell them even more patriotically and, where possible, incite them to a patriotic hero's death. We patriots are left with no other recourse but to become Communists to prevent the enemy from becoming even more Communist, and drowning our patriotism in sheer communism."

"Sirs," said War Minister von Fungusbeard, "Communist Liebrecht is a puppet manipulated by others behind the scenes. By whom, you ask? Believe me, the German National Party is subsidizing hoopla.[70] It wants to draw negotiations out."

Finally, the cabinet agreed that they had to work on two fronts.

Firstly, against the enemy, by representing the national conscience. Secondly, to carefully build a bridge to the Communist party, which might in the near future become the next government.

With this agreement, the cabinet returned to the hall. Emil Blender ascended the lectern and, in an effort to respond to the Communists, began his inaugural speech as follows:

"Honored Sirs! The previous speaker has parroted the general Communist party line that we know only too well. We don't want to argue about style and good taste here. Expressions such as 'bastards' haven't, until now, been acceptable in the cultured society of Europe's chosen intellects. Perhaps a new *Kultur* is coming, perhaps none at all is preferable."

("Bravo!" from the right of the platform).

"Far be it from us to underestimate the justification of the previous speaker's charges. We understand the patriotic sentiments of our Communist compatriots. Indeed, we *share* these feelings. Let this be a warning writing on the wall to you, honored sirs, who are forced back and constrained by the enemy's chassepots and cannons. Our nation, split apart into ten regions and twenty-eight political parties is, at this moment, totally *unified* in its *essential needs*."

("Bravo!" from the left of the platform).

"But let us not forget the *other* part of the Communist program: the noble thoughts and truths of Christian salvation. The main thing is for us to give the crowd waiting outside a satisfactory answer, which will make them go home and allow us to leave."

("Bravo!" this time even from the French side).

Then something surprising happened. Boche stood up and said, with honest modesty and devoted martial spirit: "Let us pray!"

Cardinal Nitti, in violet stole, accompanied by two bishops, stood before the assembly. Altar boys swayed censers to and fro. The room was fragrant with incense.

Nitti began: "Brothers and sisters in Jesus Christ, Lamb of God who took on Himself all the sins of the world by dying under Pontius Pilate. In the name of the Father, the Son, and the Holy Ghost. In this decisive hour when death hangs over us and a new epoch begins, let us call to Lord Jesus: let HIM illuminate our lives."

Grand Old Man Tünnes cursed. Cannon Thiessen cursed. Coalkrupp cursed. All the politicians, bankers, and industrialists cursed, "That rascal," thought Foreign Minister Emil Blender. But they all folded their hands, and recited the Our Father with fury in their hearts. The out-of-towners smirked insolently. They perceived Faussecocheur's shrewd manipulation. He had saved the day once again by using ideas to "counteract" the Communists' turbulent national ideas with a few well-chosen counter ideals of his own.

Hands folded over belly, smug in his spotless conscience, Faussecocheur twisted his small piggy-eyes.

Monsignor Nitti raised the cross and blessed the assembly.

"Kitschy" said Heini, on the left side of the platform. (reflecting a free-thinking past).

Tomi, who knew Heini's point of view beforehand, said to the literary Ephebes around him: "This was indeed a solemn moment. But I still believe in the occult…"[71]

In Aeschylus's Oresteia, when Oedipus, old, blind, and abandoned by the gods, stands in front of the abyss into which the Sphinx has plunged, he cries out, astonished at the ways of fate:

"And so, without knowing it, I returned to the place I had come from."[72]

That was exactly how Liebrecht felt. He stared into the hall's abyss without understanding why he was so generally acclaimed. After all, he had done nothing but spew hate, bile, and vengeance.

How did this all happen?

At 6.00 am that morning, he had planted himself on the forest edge with nothing but three slices of brown bread and a small piece of sausage in his pocket.

He had stood there for five hours in the company of women, old men, and cripples.

Fantastical figures appeared before him, saying "We must organize the defense of the fatherland!" The words "general strike" were repeated again and again. The crowd, always inclined towards high-minded feelings, sang patriotic songs. But he resisted. He had never been unfaithful to the ideal of supranational "worker's solidarity."

National enthusiasm[73] is like influenza. No matter how long one shelters from it, infection surely follows.[74]

He thought of his hedgerow garden and the apple trees. Two days ago they had burned it down, and with that he had been plunged into sudden sorrow

Then Tünnes the Younger spoke. He was beloved by everyone.

Something never experienced before rose up inside of him. Perhaps the soul of previous generations, perhaps the soul of the earth itself.

In short, he dashed forward and embraced his political rival as a brother.

The people cheered and carried them both aloft. Tünnes rushed in to fill the gap as one of his party's leaders, and straightaway proposed a plan to destroy all machines, all mine tunnels, to compel the enemy to withdraw.

Everything was non-political and ridiculous at the same time. The complex current situation had placed both himself and *this* plan at the head of his party.

But now, when Liebrecht was raised up, he saw in clear, sharp focus that his patriotic conduct was a mistake.

It was an excellent political chess gambit but, provided truth remained truth, everything descended into lunacy. He had expected to find two nations in a wrestling match. Instead, he only saw competing groups of traders, pitting class against class. Whether he could haul the chestnuts out of the fire for either Tünnes the Elder or Boche, remained to be seen.

For the first time in his life, Jens Liebrecht felt that the entire sphere of public life was nothing but theater.

No one believed in each other's feelings, but all played the game and forced one another to play. However, on the stage *life* is "very different." Nobody gets wet when it rains on a theater; the forest doesn't grow, lightning doesn't set anything ablaze.

They say "humanity" but don't mean living humans. They say "fatherland" but don't mean the apple tree from whose branches our youth hew their wanderlust.

They love and hate. Is that a *lie*? It would be foolish even to ask. Does the actor feel the role that he plays? Or does he perhaps feel *nothing*?

Liebrecht was anguished by yet another question: Was he too straightforward for the world? Was it too straightforward for him?

The latter seemed more likely. People are nurtured on goals, like flowers climb up fences, and are too simple for life's diversity.

They have one weapon, by which everything is created and achieved. They call it *history*. Reality, history, time…all seemed mechanical to him. Man is an objectified animal. By the mere fact of living, he *determines* experience. People see things as through a mirror. They are filmed while the battle is taking place, and this morning's wound can be reviewed in the cinema the same evening. And so, they murder their *life* with their history.

If a Moses appeared who cursed his people and shattered the work of his own hands, the people would cheer their own downfall, secure in the knowledge that they would thereby fall into the clutches of those who could kill them.

If God came down to earth again to offer his life up for the people's sins, oh what business they would make selling entrance tickets for his execution! They would found a culture, a book, a church on its basis. Theater: Ever and again: theater!

What did they want, in all seriousness? God in Heaven! They all agreed on one thing: "Wine is better than beer, and champagne is better than wine" He, Jens Liebrecht, had fallen into the trap—the great ideological swindle.

He stood victorious. But what a hollow victory! Never had he felt more deceived or cheated. Never had he despised himself more. He had betrayed the ostracized of the earth. He was no victor—he was a traitor.

He spat on the fatherland. The fatherland disgusted him. He wanted no fatherland.

While a cold disgust washed over him like an icy bath, a strange voice bubbled forth from him like lava from a volcano. It wasn't the voice of his own blood, but rather the voice of disappointment, of his *awareness*.

He screamed into the hall:

"This plant had to grow in the dark. It too could have blossomed. It too could have given forth the sweet fragrances of the earth. But it was told: 'You don't belong in the garden plot. Into the cellar with you.' And so it grew in the dark. But every plant *must* strive for light. Therefore, it repeatedly put forth its long white sprouts, those long, sick fingers of yearning, until it reached window and sun. But then its pale branches were cut down. Despite all, it finally reached the window and, while dying, gave forth its late, tender blossoms and modest fragrance.

"That was this morning! I finally reached the saving window and, for the first time in my life, affirmed something.

"It isn't blood that forces us to be deniers. You yourselves have *made* me into a denier.

"Healthy life protects itself. Healthy life strikes *back* when it is struck. Give me faith! You leaders of the nation, give me faith!

"What do we wish to say to the betrayed waiting outside? Away with the enemy! Out of our country! Else everything that I have wanted is deception. I call out today what I called out yesterday:

"Down with European society! It's ripe for death anyway! *Decide*!"

He fell silent. It was if the Phoenix appeared at noon in the Berlin stock exchange and sang to the assembled commerce councilors about the myth of the sun god Ra.[75]

Politicians, bankers, ladies, intellectuals, soldiers—all stared helplessly. But this only lasted for a few minutes. Then—thunderous applause resounded.

The foreign minister was most satisfied of all.

"You see," he said to Kuno Reisser, "he is one of the most adroit politicians we have ever met. His natural attitude is moronically naïve. He works with the well-known bouquet of ideological idiom and folksy aphorisms. By so doing he pursues his goals step by step, and uses the opportunity to plunge us into as much confusion as possible. But *I* am the only one he cannot hoodwink. I see confirmation of my original opinions. His patriotic presentation was just a charade. The party chose this path for him, to blacken its name with us. Now the man sits in the driver's seat and is already trying to change the program, by leaving the way to old principles open. At the right moment, he will become a Communist again."

"Yes" said Kuno Reisser, "politics is the correct middle ground between extremes. Stupid people flounder, clever ones find the correct balance."

"*We*, however," added Blender, "announce a four-week general strike. Then Boche and Faussecocheur will be for it: intruders, bloodhounds, pigs!"

Again, our sensitive local statesmen would have had less hatred in their hearts for our archenemies, had they heard what Faussecocheur said to his friends:

"I still say that the man is a patriot and an idiot at the same time. Believe me, Marshal, communism is only a matter of intelligence. But intelligence is unnatural. People are innately patriotic; therefore they can be *dealt with*."

The foreign minister begged leave to speak. Blender began:

"The government has the following answer to comrade Liebrecht's valiant words: Plants born in the dark (to borrow the previous speaker's gracious metaphor) only blossom in the sunlight of achievement. We rejoice when that occurs! We shall not disappoint our Communists' worthy faith in the government's heroic resistance. We declare a general strike for the entire Ruhr area, as long as the *external* enemy remains on our land. We recognize no internal enemies anymore. The leader of the Internal Communist Party's strong and honorable personality guarantees that we will close ranks in *a common front against foreign domination* unswervingly and with all our strength.—"

Had Jens Liebrecht not tried to be cleverer than he really was at that moment and shut his mouth, he would doubtlessly have become "one of Europe's leading lights." He would have been able to serve his people and party as he wished, thanks to his great potential and many talents. But instead, he interpreted his confused private feelings in so nonsensical a way, that the future course of events remained completely unclear.

The main issue was that he was very ashamed of himself. He had placed himself in the position of a man who is successful in everything because everything he says and does is totally misunderstood. Out of a vortex of conflicting feelings (rage, contempt, compassion, responsibility, astonishment, pain, laughter), a nagging self-recrimination "you are guilty before your own conscience" repeatedly surfaced. Half out of a frenzy of contempt that blew himself and his fatherland to pieces, half out a consciousness of demanding the utmost from himself, he began to speak again. He had no idea whether he spoke with his heart's voice or with a foreign voice from books.

"You always speak of an 'enemy in the country!' Yes! We *have* an enemy in the country. Around me sit the select leaders of our hemisphere, the world's great intellects."

(From the right, Cry-Baby the Ephebe cried "Bravo!" but, from the left, Manny Shakespeare the Corybant warned "Pst!").[76]

With a grand gesture that encompassed the entire hall, he cried out: "*Here* is the country's enemy!"

"Oho!" from intellectuals on the platform.

"Yes, all these are the country's enemy."

(A call which became dangerous to the speaker echoed from the back benches: " Isn't this hogwash, Wilhelm?" Several started to laugh).

Liebrecht ploughed on:

"*Enemy* in the country. So much for your damned cleverness, your noble minds, your economy, your politics.

"*Enemy* in the country... he who patronizes other people with his education., his technology, his knowledge, his ability.

"*Enemy* in the country.... he who kills the earth's soul.

"*How* does he kill the earths soul? By turning it into work, into spirit, into matters and things, space and time, history and progress. By objectifying it and turning it into coin. Where *is* your soul? What work that you perform testifies to your *being*?[77] Where does the elemental cross over into the sphere of *the word*?

"*Enemy* in the country...He who imposes norms and ideals, the insanity of logic, on God-given nature.

"*Enemy* in the country...one who teaches others to improve the world, to raise humanity up. Because everything is self-righteousness, self-interest, will to power,[78] swindling. The world's all title page there's no content.

"*Enemy* in the country...someone who cloaks himself in humility. Because darkness cloaks itself in humility, kneels down and says 'God, enlighten us!'

"The *enemy* is the spirit that murders simplicity and the flower and animal world.

"Only now do I understand that I stand before you like a real blockhead."

("Very true" from the gallery. Others warned: "Pst!").

"Yes, *meine Herren*, "I *am* a blockhead, a man of the proletarian masses. I don't understand you!"

("Yeah. Thus spoke Zarathustra," a derisive heckler chimed in.[79] Others called: "let him spill all his beans and finish already!")

"Better said: I *do* understand you, but you don't understand *me* because you're too clever by half."

General laughter.

"Most certainly! Too clever! Superior in art, the mind, politics, *Kultur*!"

Suddenly Baron von Soonwillhave's ever-cheerful baritone resounded: "Meschugge is trump!"

Liebrecht continued imperturbably:

"I know exactly what you think of me: I am *crazy*."

General laughter. But Blender whispered in Tünnes's ear: "Either the man is *really* mad, or he is the most cunning politician of all time." Tünnes replied: "Perhaps both!"

"*Meine Herren*! You'll presently find me very reasonable. One sign from me, and the crowd will storm the building.

"Three hundred thousand cannons are untouchable! Soldiers will desert! The people have artillery! Prepare to die! This building will soon burn! Europe will be blown up!"

His voice broke...

An awful silence froze the room solid for several minutes. No one moved a muscle: they sat stiff and dumbfounded. Then they started to move. People spoke to each other confusedly. A mocking smirk appeared on some faces, others saw the smirk and took it up. Laughter competed with fear: both were infectious. Suddenly, mortal fear burst like an air bubble, and liberating laughter streamed through the entire hall.

The folly of all this prattle was apparent! What did this man really want? There were two possibilities: Either he was mad, or satan personified.

But no...A third possibility could explain everything. He was a literary personality. Perhaps a disciple of Alfred Kerr, Bernard Shaw, Carl Sternheim, or Theodor Lessing.[80] One had to assume that everything was just a piece of interesting literature. Then it all became simple and natural.

The only one who still misconstrued everything morally was little Mannheimer. His abrasive voice rang out through the hall: "This is exactly how the *truth* looks!"

"No—no," platform dignitaries called out, laughing.

Luckily, the spiritual rock-crushers resumed their restless grinding, bringing everything into the correct balance.

The marginal glosses of word history formulate cultural judgments: It has ever been so. Mirrors reflect. Windmills clack. Rushing water turns waterwheels to and fro. Grain becomes wheat flour ready for the ovens. Cataracts of words flow. The brain facilitates "correct orientation."

In the Imperial box, Perponcher said to Prinzheimer: "The young man is a little too subjective, but not totally unlikeable." Prinzheimer, powdering the tip of her red nose, opined: "He will soon give a lecture on his Weltanschauung in my salon."

Cry-Baby expounded the following:

"Talk about the 'alienating principle' seems too intimate. It highlights the expressionistic self-squandering of spiritual exhibitionism. But it's nevertheless easy to see that *he* too is an artist—a man with literary more than political ambition."

After Manny Shakespeare heard the historical mindset of his opposite number, he offered the following wise words:

"I regret absence of the primal scream...,I will be understood in select circles when I say that we lack the immediate demonic possession of Wälsung incest.[81] We are burdened with too much bourgeois ideology. Radicalism can be either genuine or artificial. As for me, I would hang myself on Ygdrasil the world tree the day I discover a *more* radical spirit than *my own* in Germany.[82] I will soon write an essay on genuine radicalism which I will publish in the *Neue Deutsche Rundschau*.[83] I will read it to the proletariat, and in the patriotic women's club 'Befreundete Helden 1914,' with entry tickets priced for popular demand."

When culture (by way of literature) finds entries and explanations for the unconventional behavior of a communist chieftain who has gone quite mad, industrialists stand before it like ducks in a thunderstorm.

"D'you understand this hullabaloo?" Cannon Thiessen asked. "What does this bozo want?"

"What he wants?" the grand old man answered, "*world revolution*, of course!"

Baron von Soonwillhave replied: "nebbish."[84]

(Because his party tipped the scales, it was always easy for them to smile at such political partiality).

Even Emil Blender gradually become unsure of himself. He said to Chancellor Reisser: "I suspect that the political aims pursued here are beyond even *me*. It seems that this individual is playing the silly fool in a way that has become unnatural."

The minister of culture put in his five cents worth: "Dear Blender, do you know about the Dada movement?[85] Modern Dadaist politics have thrown the old school propagandistic media overboard. The good old traditions of national business and cameral and cabinet diplomacy don't apply anymore. One only works with emotion. But isn't this man *crazy*?"

"He's a politician all the same," said Blender thoughtfully.

Faussecocheur was of the opposite opinion:

"My knowledge of people," he said to Boche, "doesn't deceive me for a moment. I tell you that this man is much too *naïve* to be a patriot. He is merely a primitive sheep, a gentle idiot useful only for a small Bible wreath, a Christian youth association, or the Salvation Army."

Views of the esteemed local philosophers in the assembly were very complicated.

Schnitzelmaker said:

"As a psychologist, I hold the entire issue to be mad, but beg to differentiate between acted and faked, and so-called natural madness. The issue is simple. Shakespeare portrays Hamlet as playing the fool, without actually proving that he really *isn't* mad.[86] One puts on a mask of stupidity in order to hide one's own stupidity.

"Observe two things: First, the politics of communism is half faked, half real nonsense. Its faked nonsense has a purpose, and is therefore sense. By contrast, naïve nonsense is irrational as madness.[87] Secondly, the human experience that breaks through the outer shell of consciousness into the subconscious level of the irrational, in other words into the mystical-metaphysical, is in reality an experience of *fear*. And so I can say: when real nonsense exceeds deliberate nonsense, it manifests itself in a certain amount of proletarian fear. It follows, that the proletarian is neither a man of courage nor a man of action.[88] For scientific reasons, the renaissance of men of action is long overdue. Someone like Liebrecht will *not* bring it about, but people like Cecil Rhodes, Tünnes, and other audacious men will"

Count Klingaling, the self-absorbed Darmstadt life-seeker, chimed in:

"Dear colleagues: General polarity of the rightly admired antithesis—here is nature, here soul, here spirit—has been described in many learned philosophical books. But this polarity only exists insofar as the rhythm of the irrational *makes itself aware* as consciousness in space and time while, beyond the world of conscious harmony, it's opposite—sense or nonsense—loses its nonsense.[89] Thus, I believe that Liebrecht must not be taken platonically-phenomenologically—as you, my dear Schnitzelmaker, have so insightfully asserted—but as a *unique*, living time experience, affiliated with no 'type' or 'idea.' Because only the lively life of the most lively *life* is the living *sense* of lively lived life."[90]

Schnitzelmaker had hardly began his response "Trade, trade, trade," when something happened which caused all faces to turn white as chalk, all knees to knock together,[91] and all mouths to become dumb.

The inscrutable man on the platform calmly held a mysterious object over his head, and showed it to the assembly.

It was a bomb.

Everyone now understood his meaning clearly.

He brandished it, crying:

"Long live the world revolution!"

It sounded half exultation, half *cri de coeur*.

"When morning dawns, a new spring will dawn for the new generation!"

Everyone froze. In a moment all assembled politicians overlooked the connection. Soviet Russia, America, India, China, Australia, the entire world proletariat stood behind the bomb. The hour of world revolution, so often announced, had arrived unexpectedly.

Faussecocheur was the only one who still doubted:

"Quick, Marshal," he whispered, "crawl under the chair, *découvrez le communisme et vous verrez le patriidiotisme* [uncover communism, and you'll find patrio-idiocy]."

No soon had the initial shock subsided, when all hell broke loose.

People crowded around doors and tried to jump out of windows. A black mass of people stood in front of doors and windows. All exits were blocked, and the defending forces did not resist. The *Volk* surged around the walls, and threatening voices were heard from all sides.

Women in the stands yelled and swooned.

Heini lay in the left hand gallery: the best surgeons in the country held opodeldoc[92] under his nose. Tomi lay to his right. No matter how the two brothers' Weltanschauung differed, their souls were cosmically *identical.* They both agreed that neither could smell any gunpowder. But one fact burdened their end with soul-wrenching tragedy: Their brains, exploited by too many of our literary masterpieces, searched frantically but in vain for a "last word" with which they could pass into literary history.

At this fateful moment, only one man had a positive, redemptive instinct.

It was *Guschen*!

Guschen to the rescue! That valiant statesman saved everyone's life!

Only simple natures are suitable as father figures. God can only speak humanly and like a *human* through Balaam's ass.[93]

Guschen stood up, walked up to Liebrecht gingerly, and said:

"At this most difficult hour of my life, I surrender my office to you…may you (he added out of associative custom) may you consider that we carry the responsibility for all unborn generations before the bar of world history."

With that, he shoved the dangerous bomb into a pocket in his Prussian blue topcoat.

The nightmare was averted.

The assembly calmed down. *Kultur* and civilized humanity were once again graced by the two brothers Mann,[94] returned to life.

However, what happened now was so confused, so colorful, and so baffling, that it isn't possible to integrate events in chronological order.

I beg the reader to consider that everything a historian reports sequentially is often concentrated into a single short second.

What exactly happened and how?

Hardly had the assembly calmed down, when Marshal Boche de Trocadero emitted a gruesome shout of rage. He jumped up, face purple with fury, screaming: "Dogs! I'll make you all pay for this! Dogs! You'll pay for this!"

It seemed as if his martial spirit had become infected with a sudden attack of rabies.

Beside him, Guschen Ehrlich rolled around on the floor.

The moment he saw the bomb, Boche had—on Faussecocheur's advice—crawled under a leather armchair. From this vantage point, he saw how Guschen had put the bomb in his coat pocket and heard him, on his own authority, name Jens Liebrecht as head of the (now-defunct) German Empire.[95] He didn't understand German properly and the day's events had started to confuse his straightforward soldier's mind. He felt betrayed, imagining that everything had been a put-up job, and suspected that Guschen wanted to grab the government for himself. In short, the situation misled Boche into hurling all sorts of terrible insults. Guschen was certainly no politician, but the tone that he struck was not a lightweight one. Additionally, the self-assurance of a man carrying a bomb in his pocket is not to be taken lightly. In short, Guschen also started to roar, and boxed Boche's ears severely. In a moment, the tremendous patriotic tension that had hovered over these overexcited, bewildered people since early morning was vented in the most fearful way. An ear-splitting row resulted, and scuffles with, words—and unfortunately also fists—broke out.

As said, this was all the process of an instant.

At the same moment, wild and violent incidents—whose causes weren't clear even after the event—broke out *outside* the hall.

Strange rumors that the Communists had seized power from the government by coup d'état did the rounds amongst the masses in Dollarcamp. World revolution was supposed to have been proclaimed in the Great Hall of the People, and Liebrecht was voted in as dictator of the proletariat in Guschen's place.

Windows were smashed and doors forced open. Stairs and passages were stormed and occupied. The few guardsmen hardly resisted.
The mob was already in the building. New crowds of people tried to
get in, pushing in from the outside. They were led by a deputation of
Communist workers tasked, in the name of the working masses, to
demand *proof* of the repeal of the Treaty of Falsiloques and departure of
the enemy occupation army.

These delegates burst through the great oak doors, arriving in the
hall at the same moment Guschen and the marshal were having the row.

Faussecocheur saw the changed situation in an instant. He knew
exactly how to quickly cover up the deputies' potentially disastrous first
impression on the workers. It was very simple: he stood on a chair, and
powerfully intoned "La Marsellaise."

The politicians, recognizing the danger, helped him from all sides.
They took out their pocket handkerchiefs, waved them over their heads
towards the workers, and immediately began to plant the seeds of fraternité.

Tünnes had the admirable presence of mind to cry: "Long live the
eight-hour day!"

In anguish, Cannon Thiessen began to sing: "Blood must flow,
blood must flow, down with the capitalist dogs!"

The workers acted somewhat slow-wittedly to the general chaos.
But their wild over-excitement turned patriotic fury and tension into
the Dionysian ecstasy[96] of a more *socially*-oriented enthusiasm. As a
result, many didn't know whether they should beat up the opposition,
or embrace them as brothers.

Everyone knew one thing: death hovered over the gathering. If
the proletariat were *not* calmed down, all would be lost. Everything
depended on giving the invading proletarians the assurance that their
wishes would be granted!

Packed masses of people bulged through doors and windows

"Youngsters," those inside called, "please be so kind as to remain
outside. We will come out, and celebrate the spring of revolution
together with you surrounded by the beauty of nature. Then the new
world era will begin"

Tünnes the Younger again proved himself to be the nation's blond darling. He kissed each of the Communist delegates in turn and pushed himself outside through the door.

Guschen and Boche were squeezed onto the Great Balcony by force. Parliament demanded that, as representatives of both nations, they show unity with the working masses. They were urged to embrace and kiss each other in full view of the crowds.

Photographers readied their cameras. Representatives of Ufa, the largest international movie company in Germany,[97] prepared to film the world-shaking event.

It became evident that politicians had judged the national spirit correctly. The frenzied crowd calmed down when the famous great heads of European politics appeared on the balcony. They presented the image of national reconciliation in plain view to the crowd in profoundly moving fashion.

Boche and Guschen behaved like two hard mouthed young foals who didn't submit to political necessity and wanted to enforce public policy themselves. They played hard to get in every possible way.

"*You* start, please," Boche whispered poisonously. Guschen, who would have preferred to throw the bomb and strangle Boche, responded biliously: "I kiss you only under duress." This *really* was one of the most difficult hours of his life, not just his usual blather.

But finally, because there was no alternative, the Head of the German (non-existent) Empire embraced the enemy general. The manipulated *Volk* stood reverently, men with bared heads. Mothers, accustomed to constant cares, raised their children high, to see and never forget this world-historical hour.

"Ow," said Boche, "your beard is scratching me. Please, sir, pray tone down your brotherly kisses."

(Afterwards, Guschen asserted that, while embracing, Boche had pinched him, to prove his duplicity. By contrast, Boche asserted that Guschen was too fat to embrace properly).

And so, sad to say, history's representatives hurled abuses at each another, while the *Volk* enjoyed the pseudo-reconciliatory performance of two noble cultures, by the light of the setting sun.

Guschen and Marshal, Tünnes the Elder and his counterpart Faussecocheur, appeared on the balcony. Everyone knew that both men had concocted the Economic Agreement of Monte Carlo together. There, they had agreed on what they saw as the correct division of crude oil and petroleum sources, coal, and ores, on which the world's cultural and heroic history depended.

Faussecocheur cried: "Hurrah for the eight-hour day!" and pointed to Tünnes, as if he alone deserved credit for introduction of this new benefit. Tünnes returned the favor, calling out: "Hurrah for right-wing politics and honesty," pointing to his counterpart.

Faussecocheur placed his arm familiarly on the old man's bull neck and softly tickled his collar. In return, Tünnes took Faussecocheur's fat head and, pushing his face against the Frenchman's ear, whispered softly: "You're a *rascal*." Faussecocheur elegiacally replied: "You're *right* about that, Tünnes."

The *Volk* surged onto the balcony. How did our noble German poet Walter Bloem so beautifully put it?[98]

"The sinking red of the May sun was reflected in drops of pearly tears, wept aloft from the depths of young German men and maiden's mourning hearts. But Kleio the Muse, in blood purple garment, opened a new page in humanity's book of fate, and wrote *Europe's Rebirth* on a new page with an iron pen."[99]

Then, the *Volk* demanded to see and hear from Foreign Minister Blender and Culture Minister Gabbler.

Blender was ready. As proof of brotherliness he chose Mannheimer as his opposite number, and asked him to accompany him onto the balcony. Mannheimer received the request shyly, saying:

"I appear before you like an enchanting lady at a cotillion, received on all sides with bouquets. I don't know why you have chosen *me*. Please choose someone worthier—I am already pledged to Kuno Reisser."

But Blender insisted on Mannheimer. If this ridiculous kissing charade really was necessary, Mannheimer remained the most likable candidate.

And so the *Volk* were treated to the strange spectacle of national banking in the person of Mannheimer, and national politics in the person of Blender, kissing and embracing each other. Even on this occasion, however, Mannheimer refused to take the cigar out of his mouth.

The *Volk* now demanded the appearance of Jens Liebrecht and Baldur Tünnes. But Liebrecht was nowhere to be found, and this almost led to catastrophe. Baldur came out alone, saying that Liebrecht was far too busy drafting the "dictatorship of the proletariat" to be able to appear with him.[100] He was thus able to strew the obstruction caused by Liebrecht's disappearance with roses, particularly because so many celebrities from in and outside the country showed the people living examples of redemption and reconciliation.

Thus, the combined leadership of Europe converted to both pacifism and communism. They were left with no alternative, because of the threat of being trampled or hanged by the revolutionary mob.

European reconstruction along the lines of Communist people's government having become a reality, intellectuals decided to respond to the "call of the modern era" by reconciling with one another. Their right and left spiritual wings were represented by Messrs. Manny Shakespeare and Cry-Baby, respectively.

As a result of much negotiation, the two literary brothers appeared ready to celebrate their reconciliation with a public embrace, thereby making the riches of a new cultural epoch available to the *Neue Deutsche Rundschau, Meyers Konversationslexikon*,[101] and Gundelfinger's literary history[102] for the very first time.

After much fussing with their cravats before the mirror, Tomi and Heini, accompanied by their cultural circle (Venetian Ephebes and Maenads, respectively),[103] walked in solemn procession from right and left side to the balcony. They presented their noble profiles to the setting golden-red spring sun and adorned each other with a hallowed kiss. Tomi (who had meanwhile become a free German republican) expounded the document as follows: "The spiritual unification aim of the general international rational state will blossom based on the national foundation of our natural differences." Heini (who had developed a more moderate nationalist approach) answered passionately: "Just the opposite! We will construct the national state based on natural personal differences, on the unifying foundations of the international spirit."

The importance of this day exceeded even 4 August 1789 and 4 August 1914, those two glorious days in world history.[104]

In August 1789, everyone decided to become citizens of the world; in August 1914 they decided the exact opposite.

Today, everyone became everything *at one stroke*: Communist, Bolshevik, individualist, democrat, aristocrat, and everything else imaginable. Not only the nobility, but also better paid democrats, renounced all their prerogatives.

Baron von Soonwillhave was the first to declare that he would from now on shed his nobility and be satisfied with the modest name "Cohn."[105]

And so, everything succeeded. The people were calmed down, danger eliminated. The mood of the proletarian masses in Dollarcamp gradually shifted to something like a North German shooting match, a South German Oktoberfest, a Rhenish carnival.

But more embarrassment loomed.

The victorious Communists put forth specific requirements. They refused to give up their siege of the Great Hall of the People and encirclement of Europe's cultural representatives, until four demands were met.[106]

Firstly: The assembly must immediately decide to evict the foreign occupation army from German soil. This decision must be put in writing and shared with the people. Secondly: connection with the ten divisions of the occupation army must remain cut until Boche and Faussecocheur order disarming of the soldiers and transfer of the artillery to the people. Thirdly: Communist delegates must attend negotiations, which must begin immediately under Jens Liebrecht's leadership. If no satisfactory conclusion could be reached then, fourthly, the "dictatorship of the proletariat" must immediately be installed.

What was to be done?

Things were so determined that the Communist Spring Charade had to be played out until it pleased the louts to finally go home and to bed. If the gods of this world don't have a free path to their cannons, they are de-deified. They were nothing but hostages in the hands of the proletariat, with whom they had to fraternize, for good or ill. Now, only one hope remained: that even proletarian leaders preferred cigars to bloodshed.

They all now reckoned on Liebrechts's good-naturedness, and left him as sole helmsman of the muddled ship of state. Everyone was delighted at not having to take any responsibility for it at this stage.

"Let's make the lyrical Balduin Bählamm *dictator*," Faussecocheur said to Tünnes.[107] "He'll order the wolves to eat[108] clover in the future. *On ne sort jamais impunément de son caractère* [one cannot escape one's nature with impunity]. The young man is not dangerous, but rather morally depraved: I mean depraved *because of* morals. We should always revere ethics. Virtue is a woman: the more one pursues it, the easier one gets rid of it. The main thing is to escape from this damn stable."

But Liebrecht was nowhere to be seen: disappeared, evaporated, washed away! Just as abruptly as he had surfaced that morning, and just as enigmatically.

Guschen Ehrlich, who had unavoidably climbed back into the Presidential Seat of Honor, said bitterly: "In my opinion, *this* is his *greatest* disgrace of all."

Emissaries were sent out to search for Liebrecht. They were tasked with returning him to the Great Hall of the People at all costs dead or alive, kicking and screaming if necessary, because only *he* could control the mob and release the assembly from their involuntary imprisonment.

In the meanwhile, they tried to renegotiate constitutionally, in the presence of Communist representatives.

Everything had to be postponed. Before, each party of the packed and gullible horde had been played one against the other, to obtain the greatest benefit for those inside. But now, the assembly silently agreed that their priority was to emerge from the grisly hall alive, and send the

mob on their way satisfied with the outcome. This wish led to a concilia-
tory, congenial, fraternal atmosphere among all present.

The politicians tried to play each into the other's hands for the general good. Faussecocheur filed proposals through Tünnes, and Tünnes
through Faussecocheur.

Firstly, Tünnes (really Faussecocheur) proposed land reform.
Everything in Dollarcamp—the Great Hall of the People, pits, factories,
smelters—must immediately be declared public property. This of course
included the great wine cellars underneath the Great Hall, in which Tünnes
the Elder stored his noble stash of Rhine and Mosel wines, old cognacs,
and delectable red burgundies. The keys to the wine cellars were immediately delivered to the Communist Party. Several delegates rushed to "examine" their booty. Faussecocheur's vile skullduggery was obvious to everyone
except Tünnes. He filed the motion (tantamount to a giant endowment)
with a sweet-sour face and accepted the beneficiaries' thanks with con-
cealed rage. One can understand and sympathize with his situation. For
me personally, nothing could be more bitter than being compelled by my
enemies to declare my wine cellar communal property, just for spite.

Secondly, Faussecocheur (in reality Tünnes, who hoped in this way
to take revenge on Faussecocheur) moved for the relevant paragraphs of
the new international treaty to be discussed immediately in committee,
then submitted to the Communists for editing and approval.

But, in reality, everyone's thoughts revolved around only *one thing*:
how do we get troops to the Great Hall? How do we scatter these ruf-
fians outside to the four winds?

The historical context of events had in the meantime become so
complicated that no amount of human ingenuity could keep track
of their causality. The most important piece of the puzzle remained
unsolved: where was Liebrecht? Where was he? What had he wanted?
Was he patriot or Communist? Who were the people behind his timely
appearance and just as timely disappearance?

Because world history is far too complex for my meager intellect, I
have turned to Herr Erich Marcks, a Berlin historian, and asked him to
clarify the issue in one of his seminars.[109]

The incomparable brilliance of our German school of history has provided me with an Ariadne-like thread with which to navigate through its labyrinthine complexities.[110] I don't believe myself justified in withholding this German historian's learned exposition from the honored reader.

Herr Erich Marcks wrote me the following:

"It must be well known to you, greatly honored sir, that the Battle of Waterloo was not won by Wellington or Blücher, but by the Vienna banker Rothschild."[111] While the battle was taking place, Rothschild was taking a cup of coffee at the "Golden Goose" in Brussels, keeping himself abreast of the course of the battle through his informant. In this way, he was informed 30 minutes before any other mortal man that Napoleon had no prospect of winning. He immediately circulated the news that Napoleon had prevailed on the stock exchange. At the same time he informed his banking house by predetermined ciphers that they should buy up English and German government securities (which were at the time available for a song, while French equivalents had risen to unimaginable heights). When the exchange closed an hour later, news came in that Napoleon had lost, and English and German securities— still worth practically nothing—became, in reality, the safest possible investments. Rothschild won the battle by a tactic much simpler than that of Napoleon—it was one of history's brightest days. And yet, it amounted to practically nothing compared to little Mannheimer's enormous victory.

Valued reader, allow me to go over the sequence of events again, paying special attention to Mannheimer's behavior.

All parties had played with the idea of a general strike—everyone used it as a weapon against the workers. Mannheimer quickly noticed this, and staked everything on this one issue. But while this game was too much for the others, Mannheimer won it, thanks to a simple stratagem.

After he—still sitting in his corner—had issued coded orders to all his subordinate banks, he ordered telephone communications to be cut, thereby robbing parliament—threatened now by its own cannons—of contact with the outside world. While everyone in the hall floated (or *thought* that they floated) under death's wings, everyone else in and outside the country knew of the decision to stop work for the duration of the enemy invasion. This greatly amused Mannheimer, the puppeteer manipulating events. He couldn't have cared less whether this work stoppage really happened or not. The fact was that stocks and bonds of local industries and local currency had all become worthless, and that all could be bought up for a song by Mannheimer's agents. All (and this gratified him the most) without any *other* bankers sharing the booty. Because Mandelsüß & Co. financed the general strike, this turn of events didn't have to be released to the public, nor influence international trade. In this way, Mannheimer had sunk his Jewish claws into all local industry. At the favorable moment—which he himself cunningly manipulated—he had bought out all obligations and stock certificates. But what was *Liebrecht's* role in this great game? If one didn't accept that Liebrecht and Mannheimer were in bed together and shared the booty, then one would have to accept that Liebrecht was merely a puppet, with Mannheimer pulling the strings.

Mannheimer let these ambiguous politically naïve daydreamers and sentimentalists dance and twitch on his strings until he had no more use for them and could let them disappear. In this way, he used the telephone to *create* the Communist world era. He let it run riot for a while, so long as it was useful for his transactions and profiteering, but then allowed Europe to return to its customary business, liberated from unnecessary ideology. Presumably, he wished to change Germany into a federation of twenty-five autonomous regions, appealing to national rights of self-determination, old tribal consciousness, or similar swindles, while he traveled comfortably by chauffeured limousine to dine at the Adlon or Kempinski.[112]

According to the Great German Historian Marcks, this confluence of events proved that capitalism and socialism, communism and expropriation acted in concert, kept in check by learned German professorial supervision.

I believe that this description of events is clear and complete.

Under normal circumstances these ideas could have been easily transferred to academic historians such as Ranke and Treitschke, teachers and textbook writers, and generations of school children. A process of "understanding" an essentially chaotic event. Except that something else occurred which made it impossible to interpret, even for the fellow who had come up with the outlandish story in the first place and wrote a much-maligned book about *History as Giving Meaning to the Meaningless.*[113]

We were faced with one of Bismarck's famous "imponderables."[114]

Something inexplicable had occurred in the soul of Jens Liebrecht, the screwy Communist chieftain. This man who had almost singlehandedly, and with the most honest patriotism, brought about a Communist victory, had now—at the very moment of his party's triumph—*seceded* because of inner scruples and gone over to the National People's Party.[115] This is what happened:

When the frenzied fraternization began, everyone slobbered over everyone else under threat of terror, although they would much rather have strangled each another. Jens Liebrecht believed that he was witnessing realization of the Utopia for which he had striven his entire life.

Lord, preserve us from the fulfilment of our ideals! May the women whom we love not answer us. May the progress for which we strive remain a dream. If we accept that the earth changes into God's realm, what a boring world it would be! All men brothers, all free, all equal.[116] Horrible! Intolerable!

So this was the desired brotherhood of man? Yes! Is this what happens when equality and fraternity are brought about without violence and intimidation? People don't love one another spontaneously; they don't even love themselves. They only become reconciled with one another in matters of life or death, when they either stand or fall together. Otherwise it never happens!

He felt giddy! Didn't anyone think of home anymore? Was he the *only* patriot? How did the threads connect? Those who represented "national interests" advocated, negotiated, and felt internationally towards their own people. But the proletariat, who logically should have striven for "international protection" of the exploited masses, couldn't escape from national, patriotic feelings. It didn't make any sense: he couldn't believe in anyone's principles anymore, let alone his own. What a witches Sabbath! He had only *one* wish: out of here, into the fresh air, where he could see the stars at night!! Away from all this insanity!

It was difficult to believe, but true. At the exact moment when Liebrecht became dictator, he threw all his goals away. Now that he had it, he was ashamed of his success, He really didn't give a damn anymore.

He succeeded in escaping from the mass of people into a lonely field, where he crept into a bush. He saw and looked for no one, but lay on the cold ground, contemplating the slowly rising moon.

The condition of his soul was peculiar. Where was his revolutionary defiance? Where was his hate, his bile?

They had all been extinguished. And because extinguished anger is in reality the same as burgeoning love, he realized that (like the Old Testament God who alternately exterminates and loves his Chosen People) his pugnacious attitude towards the world and revolutionary fanaticism had been nothing but—a deplorable lack of indifference.

He had become sickened by too much *love* for this insignificant world. He had fretted unnecessarily over humanity and its moronic destiny.

His spirit and morals resembled thorns which tear and draw blood, but are in reality malformed buds. After all, the natural destiny of thorns would have been to bud, blossom, and emit fragrance had they not *had to* change into pointed weapons because of life-threatening cold. Perhaps *all* spirits and morals are nothing but suppressed beauty and injured love. Yes, he loved! Now, when there was no sense fighting against existing society, forcing doors that were already open; when Europe's leaders had proclaimed him *dictator*; when a wise instinct of self-preservation of a decayed society had made him judge and destroyer, *lord* of life and death (like defenseless mutts who save themselves through humble submission when they can't bark or bite anymore). Only now did he realize that he had not come to destroy, but to give, and surrender his life like Jesus Christ.[117]

So why, only minutes ago, had he desired to hurl that all-destroying bomb? Only because the world didn't want to drink from his heart's proffered chalice

But now the people's will submitted to his. Thus *he* became the responsible one. And so he became just another exponent of the law stating that all leaders only follow those whom they intend to direct.

His extinguished anger had another deeper effect, because love is more sharp-sighted than the most sharp-sighted hate. He didn't *desire* anything. He didn't want to be world führer. Certainly not! The very desire to guide the world now appeared to him like a deep, dark fault— the fault of all logical or moral demands, behind which burned the will to power of carping human reason.

So good—the world was miserable. Very good! It would have been better had there been no world. But once one already existed, it *couldn't* be any other way, else it wouldn't exist at all.

Everyone was guilty in their unspeakable stupidity and self- righteousness—grown up, spoiled children, all of them. Children, who had stumbled into a blind alley through botched culture, science, education, and spirit. But still *children, dear* children, *poor, poor* children!

All his resentment against the brokers and boasters[118] in the Great Hall had *faded away*. Now, they only seemed stupid: their very *shrewdness* was stupid. Natural jackasses like Christ, Buddha and St. Francis of Assisi[119] were so much cleverer because they didn't take themselves so seriously.

He pitied the desolate bunch of snakes, butterflies, nightingales, toads, carnivores, rodents, foxes and sheep. Each human soul comprised an entire zoo. How everything revolved around their own miserable egos! So far away from the world in which everything is important and futile at the same time[120] where the self and everyone else are both laughed at—without poison or spite.

A fantastical vision of his boyhood years appeared before him— when he was tired from work, dirty, overexerted, but his heart filled with dreams. Covetously, wrathfully and scornfully, he saw the beautiful, elegant ladies, graceful cultured poppets, floating past him in the effervescent city boulevards. It was as if he undressed them all. Off with your filmy veils! Off with your jewelry! Off with your fur coats, ermines and minks! Off with your colored, intoxicating girdles and blouses! Off with your plumes, ribbons, and lace! Off with your silken, delicate patterned stockings! Off with your rustling skirts and knickers! There they stood, shivering in their thin linen chemises. Off with the chemises as well! What is hiding behind them? Holy hell! How pitiable and unnatural you are, poor naked cultured sweeties in your deathly white pallor and cold-blooded blondness! What great tailor or upholsterer has put you together?

He dreamt that *all* humanity stood naked, robbed of their clothes and homes, their dwellings, burrows and encasements. Who betrayed man with the spectacle of so much unnatural atrophy?

People, throw the world of deed and words behind you. Discard your garments: they are not your real skin, but your shell. Now, o culture grandees, I see your naked, pathetic little souls. O sacred illusion, so far from the gods, earthlings that aren't even healthy!

With awesome objectivity—almost beyond the realm of human consciousness split into subject and object, smiling with endless, compassionate love—Jens Liebrecht, shortly to die, experienced a final unevaluable and incomprehensible epiphany. He felt lost to the hustle and bustle of world history, as if he had entered a world of almost sacred, sweetly suffused levitation. It was as if he were a solitary, risen god looking down from heaven onto earth's ant heap, not wanting, evaluating, or judging—just filled with transcendental love. Jens Liebrecht was no fighter. He was a loving man. How is love demonstrated?

True love forces weapons away from the beloved, and directs them to the one who loves, exposing himself as a sacrificial lamb. "Stab me if you can and must. I offer my blood voluntarily, to prevent further violence."

Three people are floating on a boat in a huge ocean. They are starving. They peer at one another thinking: "I could kill you." The most honest of the three says: "Here: chop my arm off, and nourish yourselves. I know you, and don't *want* to be spared myself." Could they do it? Of course they could.

It seemed to Liebrecht as if his guardian angel, his life's genius, hovered over him, whispering:

"Life and death...are not so important. World history...is not so important. Human progress...is not so important. Civilization, philosophy, science...are all not so important. Communism ...nonsense. Patriotism ...even greater nonsense. People, state, politics, history, logic, morals...are *all* nonsense. They call it love and all they bring is the evil eye. Save your soul!"

Then his soul started to speak again. That same soul that had, a few short hours ago, been so foolish as to sweep along experienced party politicians into the imprudent embrace of their arch enemy—archenemy? No! These weren't merely reflexive and mirror-men.[121] They had to love each other, because behind all their contradictions, swelled the same courage.

He felt his soul expand and become great well beyond personal will and knowledge, like the image of a lost horizon from which we spring up, only to sink back into it.

He suddenly realized that he really did have a homeland, and that all these fine people of *Volk* and *Vaterland* did not. And so he was driven to throw away the ripe fruits of his life and sacrifice them at the moment of their harvest.

Those who saw Liebrecht return to the Great Hall, greeted everywhere as bringer of a better future and national savior, attested to the fact that they had never seen such a transformation. He ascended the speaker's platform without anyone knowing that he was about to die.

He passed through the crowd luminous, serene, no trace of bellicosity—exactly the opposite of his first appearance.

His reappearance caused no astonishment. Everything else that happened that day had been so incomprehensible that no one noticed the constant situation change anymore. They hovered dreamily in a peculiar mood of vague expectation, waiting for a miraculous breakthrough that would resolve the unsustainable and preposterous position in which they found themselves. When Liebrecht arrived they thought that he would cut through the Gordian knot. But what transpired was so witless, so illogical, that no human intellect could logically justify it.

Liebrecht stepped spontaneously, confident as a sleepwalker, onto the platform. All negotiations suddenly ceased and silence reigned. They looked at him tensely and curiously, awaiting some sort of explanation or weighty announcement. But instead of that, he uttered the following words clearly and simply, with completely changed voice:

"Out with foreigners from our country! Out with foreigners from our country! Out with foreigners from our country! I say *foreigners*, because we have no enemies! Not by cannons or despicable assassination. Not by patriotic greed. Not by desire for power or international business. No! Not for the sake of all the demons of the earth, whose siblings we are. But for the sake of trees that we plant. For the sake of animals that we love. For clouds, water, winds and stones that are redeemed in our homeland's language. In sum: for the sake of the dead. Because what are trees, flowers, animals, if not the eyes of our beloved dead? What is the land we serve if not the heart and blood of all previous generations? Every clod of earth that slips through our fingers was flesh of our flesh beforehand.

"Today has taught us something. We, agents of the nation's business, have become brothers in a penned up room under the iron pressure of necessity, like strangers on a sinking ship. The deception of our petty vanities has been extinguished!

"This was merely a specter. By tomorrow everything will be blown away, only shadows and dreams will remain.

"As soon as European society, freed from entrapment between cannons and proletariat, finds itself at home in bed and well rested again, it will re-evaluate all 'interests' and 'values.' All experience will be seen as dialectic and worthless.

"And yet, this recent experience has been symbolic.

"A few hundred thousand clueless men were enough to make everyone sympathize with world revolution. We had a choice: pronounce a new historical era, or light the tinderbox and blow ourselves up. So many new historical 'epochs' have begun under the lash of necessity, but in the end nothing really changed.

"Humanity has become feverishly ill. How does a sick person help himself? He wanders restlessly from right to left, from left to right. Each time he senses relief and believes that he has found the right position. But after a few hours that position becomes unbearable, and he changes to the other side again. That is what we call 'development.'

"We humans don't love one other, we don't even love ourselves! The whole of Europe will soon resemble us in this Great Hall. The great lie of human civilization, the entire human race with its ridiculous games at the edge of the abyss, suddenly besieged by millions of frenzied, enslaved, betrayed, embittered, demanding people! The 'world revolution' will look just as it looked this evening. Just as random, just as burlesque, just as senseless…

"I realize that I stand before distinguished and important personages. Each of you is the center of his own universe! Each of you believes himself to be the harbinger of better times! I am just a poor sinner standing before high and noble people. An anti-hero amongst heroes. An ordinary man amongst geniuses. I wish from my heart that our unhappy country would, for the foreseeable future, be spared from heroes, geniuses, prophets, noble people, the illustrious and illuminated.[122] These many dashing fellows have cost us too much blood and sweat. How many countries and regions have been occupied by these great beasts of prey, only to lose them again tomorrow? How many must be discarded on the market of life so that the one can continually dine on the other? How many lives must be sacrificed, so that border posts can today be painted red, tomorrow replaced with green? How much paper is consumed daily, to wrap your garbage in the remnant of the human soul?—

"I now withdraw into the darkness of the anonymous and forgotten. All I want is to be consigned to the coffin of 'world history.' But, before I go, allow me to summarize my guiding principle in the form of a warning: you Marshal Boche and you, Master Faussecocheur—lead your mercenaries back to home and honest work. Don't unleash the demons lurking in the earth.[123] They can only be reconciled, subdued, and won over by the suffering, ploughing, seeding, growing and harvesting of a thousand loyal generations, who in the end must rest in the same earth from which their descendants' bread and beauty blossoms.

If not today, then in a paltry hundred years, the earth's demons will inexorably wrench everyone into the abyss all who, instead of loving and blessing, wish to overpower and barter it. Herr Reich President, Tünnes, Reisser, Blender, Mannheimer, and all like you in our country who want to call yourselves mighty and powerful—stop boasting about yourselves and your sons' heroic deaths at an hour when death is desecrated and becomes state business. At the very least, build on your, or someone else's, work, actions, achievements—these are the earth's *emergency exit*! Possessions and accounts are not fulfilment, expression, or traces of a human being: they destroy, objectify and instrumentalize all life. Throw away human values if they don't reflect the *soul*. We should rather destroy spirit and God, word and action, rather than become God's *slaves*."—

The effect of this speech was icy silence, mixed with fury and scorn, emotion and ridicule, disconcertment and astonishment, unease and shrugging incomprehension. They listened quietly, because they didn't have any other choice. Perhaps the scatterbrain hoped that, through his self-sacrifice, he could force others to do the same thing. Perhaps he imagined that he could convince them by his act of pride and humility.

Whatever the case was, he had made a *serious mistake*. Now everyone could see that he was useless. Every party must shake him off. He had become redundant.

One thing remained clear. The man had betrayed national politics to the Communists. Now he had again betrayed the ideals of the revolution, this time in favor of the nationalists.

Naturally! It was exactly as he said. Tomorrow, everything achieved today would evaporate like the morning dew. But, in any event, everyone's little job was secure. It was abundantly clear that Liebrecht was a patch of glue, a leech! No government could deal with such unscrupulousness. So unprincipled a man was capable of anything. *Today* he goes to bed with the Communists, *tomorrow* with the Nationalists. What does he want? Anything that is good for him. What a nerd!

Communist delegates were honestly outraged.

Their leader had turned out to be an egoist –probably a disciple of Stirner, Nietzsche, Bakunin.[124] They had achieved what they desired. They *also* sat in the catbird seats. They could smoke good cigars. They had a party wine cellar. They could have a say, join in, toot their own horn along with the others.[125] They had even swindled their way into occupying all the party seats, and a new world order to boot. A *new* cleptocracy had arisen. And now Jens Liebrecht had arrived with his sentimental Christian-Buddhist Sunday sermon and destroyed the power relationship that they had so carefully constructed!

"Treason! Treason" echoed from all benches.

It was quite obvious what the response was, and indeed *had to be.* Somehow, the assembly must get over what they had heard and change it to a healthy agenda. But who should speak?

Embarrassment was apparent on all faces.

"We, on the firm foundations of objectivity...The imperative demand of the moment...History's iron necessity...The historical significance...The political organ...We men of reality...experience, life, and Anschauung...The strong fist, healthy will...Life's golden tree... pallid theory! Utopia! Sentimentalism! Blood and iron!...etc. etc." The answer could have been so simple.

But no one took the risk,

Finally the Redeemer appeared out of Zion and the Word of the Lord from Jerusalem.

A miracle.

A round, luminescent sun orb, visible from all sides, rose triumphantly from the balcony of intellectuals. A tapeworm began to crawl forth out of the sun orb: an endless dialectical-philosophical tapeworm with a small head but long, sharp, forked tongue.

He was Schreck[126] the famous Berlin phenomenologist, and well known national ethicist.

Schreck, our academic sun, began to expound. He sounded like our good old Goethe: "The sun rolls out the same old song competing with its brother spheres."[127] His bipolar forked tongue began to rattle:

"My dear ladies and gentlemen! Anyone who listens attentively to negotiations of this eventful day and has witnessed the many deplorable interruptions of the past few hours, must have gained the impression that we are experiencing an inconceivably futile and preposterous *catastrophe*. What does it all *mean*?

"Allow me, as a representative of the school of phenomenologic analysis, to shine the pure light of logic on the nature of these events, by proper observation of the immediate situation.

"Germany's first psychologists recognized a type of mental disorder called 'circular insanity.' The disease is characterized by blind staggers or delirium tremens. Like a monkey in a cage forced to wander around *in a circle*, the patient vacillates between exaggeration and weakness, pomposity and insecurity, darkness and sentimentality, excitement and exhaustion. He seeks maniacally to insult his most honorable contemporaries in the most jealous and spiteful way (one only needs to think of the word 'bastards'). What follows is the motiveless transition into a mushy literary state of cosmic whimpering, doubly unseemly to soldiers and statesmen.

"The diagnosis is obvious. We all regret to have to pass objective judgment on so well-meaning a contemporary, but necessity demands rapid action. Even if the new era in world history remains perfect, all parties, Nationalist or Communist, are united in one thing: *the objectivity of pure recognition, the objectivity of state ethics,*[128] *as well as that of the ethical state must be subordinate to the norms of objective reason.* They may not be handed over to private psychological effusions of an arbitrary, random, unique personality. I therefore bring forward a motion…"

Schreck couldn't, and didn't need to, say anything more.

Everybody understood and recognized the threatening danger. At a single stroke, today's lunacy could be both explained and overcome by German science, normative reason, absolute logic, and objective spirit, as set forth by the all-wise, all-seeing *Schreck*:

Liebrecht wasn't only subjective, he was also pathological.

In an instant, powerful fists attacked the poor, unfortunate man and shoved a gag between his teeth, to prevent him from speaking anymore.

Only a few moments of communication were necessary.

Kuno Reisser, Blender, Tünnes, the good Reich President, the Communist leader and representatives, were all unanimous.

The windows were unbolted, and double doors torn wide open. They walked out onto the terraces and balconies in the evening twilight. The moon was already beginning to mix its dead light with the last rays of the bloodred sinking sun.

The crowd of people froze on the broad plain. They had milled around there all day, become very excited, and started to sneeze and cough. Does man live on spirit alone? No he yearns for a warm bed. No one can keep world revolution going for more than half a day.

The inscrutable moon rose. The good fat Reich President stood in the moonlight: a rubber ball pumped up with fresh hydrogen...Our Guschen, to whom we have gradually become accustomed. Behind him, rough and ready, the Grand Old Man. And Blender, Kuno Reisser, Gabbler, Thiessen, Coalkrupp, Soonwillhave, Mannheimer, all the well-known, beloved heroes of our great national epic.

The people also saw their blond favorite Baldur Tünnes, the tower, looking down at them.

But look! Oh, what a moving moment! At his bosom, like a friend clasped to his heart, *work leader Jens Liebrecht* (invisible gag in mouth).

Tünnes, with complete conviction that understood and learned from the ear of the people, began to speak:

"Brothers! Fellow-Germans! Children of our land![129] Friends! Negotiations are *completed*. Here you see your leader, *Jens Liebrecht*! He'd like to speak, but cannot, because he is completely hoarse. He has tried his best for you to the point of self-destruction. Now he can only make arm gestures. But our good Foreign Minister Emil Blender will read out to you the assembly's final decision, which will now be forwarded to the honored leaders of the Communist Party for con-formation. At the same time, 100 barrels of Rhine and Mosel wine will be siphoned off and dished out. We will all celebrate the start of a new historical epoch named '*The Reconstruction of Europe*' together on the spot!"

Emil Blender came forward, and ceremoniously read out the following treaty:

"The united representatives of the republican governments, gathered together in Dollarcamp at the Great Hall of the People, have agreed upon and obligated the following agreement:

§1. The army of occupation will leave the Ruhr region as soon as their incumbent affairs are satisfactorily settled, according to the determination and satisfaction of both parties.

§2. They will deliver twenty-seven large cannons, 123 mitrailleuses, eight-eight machine guns, 40,000 rifles, with "unmatched" models, copyrights, muskets; 10,000 bombs, 80,000 stink bombs, and order new ones from Avikage (*Allgemeine vaterländisch internationale Kannonen-Aktiengesellschaft*).

§3. One half of profits from weapons delivery must be paid into the propaganda coffers of Aaaaakavau (*Allgemeinatheistisch-anarchistisch-antinational-apolitisch-kommunistische Arbeiter-Union*)[General atheistic, anarchistic, antinational, apolitical, Communist worker's union].

§4. To achieve delivery in the shortest possible time, during the next 8 months the work day will be 12 hours, double shifts.

§5. Next Sunday, we will stage a great patriotic-Communist-political-religious, anarchistic-socialist, particularist-monist protest rally, with cooperation of the most famous leaders from both parties and established leaders of the opera.

§6. The cultural representatives of both countries will, in turn, enlighten the population on all 'modern cultural problems.' The following luminaries are earmarked for next week: Anatole France from Paris on 'The Legend of the Stork, or How Do We Tell Young Girls about Sex?'; Maximilian Harden from Berlin on 'How Do I Become Successful?'; Henri Barbusse from Tarascon on 'World Peace and the Machine Gun.' Finally, Father Amandus Polygamios Scheler from Cologne on 'How Do I become Holy?'[130]

§7. We are staging 'Inter-ethnic Love-in Evenings for Everyone, Complete with Practical Exercises' For the first evening, we have been lucky enough to obtain Mr. Raymond Poincaré, speaking on 'Bleed 'em

White'; after that Professor Moorbreaker on 'Limpdicks!' Lieutenant Ehrhardt on 'Drug Highs!'; Mr. Lloyd George on 'America Is To Blame'; Mr. Woodrow Wilson, ex-president on 'England Started It.' The concluding talk will be given by Chairman of the International Peace Association 'Amicitia' Herr Helmut von Gerlach, on 'Sex Life in Civilization.'[131]

§8. The fate of the United States of Europe will not be decided by bloody mass murder anymore, but by a system of mutual passive defiance.[132]

§9. The weapons of the new epoch will be press philosophy, general reason, German science, cinema, romance novels, theater, music, general education, and *Kultur*.

§10. Humanity will hereby change over from the iron to the paper age. The slogan of New Humanity will be, in American English, *nothing better than printing ink*. In German: our future lies in paper. Paper is made from rags, so everything on earth turns into paper. We use paper to a) Print numbers on it, thereby turning into money, which begins to count;[133] b) Print intellectual issues on it, thereby turning it into *Kultur* or the realm of values; c) To help digestion, thereby changing it into *life*.

§11. Our country will be saved by handing it over bag and baggage, together with its leading personalities, to the enemy abroad—that will be our vengeance."

Blender had finished. The wine barrels were uncorked. A tremendous Dionysian jubilation flashed through the Dollarcamp plain.

All the windows, terraces, balconies. even the dome and tower of the Great Hall, were occupied by joyful, liberated people.

The fear had passed. They were saved. Friend and foe embraced in all-loving harmony. Ladies waved perfumed handkerchiefs from the windows.

Cups and dishes were soon provided. They drank, loved, and sang. The sound of hopeful men echoed through the lovely, mild early summer evening to the enigmatic stars: "Yes, we love…we love…we love!"

The whole countrywide seemed to celebrate with them. The birds, wind and clouds sang. The soul of the world awoke, freed from specters.

The people formed one huge procession, artisans, labor unions and factories converging. Each carried his flag and emblem. Children, young boys and girls carried little flags and bands played good old patriotic songs. The train of people snaked in endless rows past the Great Hall of the People, from whose windows and balconies handkerchiefs waved. The good, fat president stood weeping crocodile tears, surrounded by the Great and the Good of *das Vaterland* and *la patrie*. Young boys carried flags and placards with inscriptions such as:

> This dawn of peace includes all others,
> We are all one great band of brothers.

> Mankind, be noble, helpful, good[134]
> Thirst not to drink your rival's blood.

> We want to be like brothers, get along,
> With German Mosel wine and German song.

> We're sure new life for all that be
> Will happen automatically.

> Organic development
> Makes old things young and young things old.

> Embrace us now we ask, dear Comrade,
> With heart and hand for fatherland

While the assembled proletarians from Dollarcamp, who had been were parading around, were finally preparing to depart, Marshal Boche and his staff had the ideal opportunity to restore Europe's military security.

Telephone communication was rapidly restored. Cannoneers could once again receive orders. Adjutants could once again be sent out through the cheerful crowds.

But the following soon became clear:

Only a very small number of troops had taken the order from head-quarters to promote a Communist putsch to heart. They had deserted, arm in arm with their blond enemies, in bars, dance halls, and cinemas of neighboring towns. They had also exchanged a small Krupp cannon, of the "my secret" model and "thick wall" patent, for two barrels of schnapps. But, in general, Faussecocheur had understood the situation correctly when he placed his trust in the patriotism of Moroccan troops. These men, used to the army's good life, and sophisticated in their culinary and drinking habits, had resisted the lure of Communism. Their true spirit of patriotism had preserved the army's discipline. Finally, although with a 2-hour detour, a new detachment was seconded to protect the Great Hall. At the same time, the gladsome tidings that fresh troop transports were expected were relayed by telephone. And so, the danger that Europe's intellectual and political elite would be boxed into the Great Hall and ground into mush by the rabble was happily avoided. Through Marshal Boche's brilliant military maneuvers, the cordon of cannons surrounding the masses was opened on four sides, to allow the satisfied, well-disposed crowd to stream homewards with no danger to anybody. For a long time, the song "Yes we love…we love….our hi-ha-homeland" echoed through the peaceful deepening night.

It was decided to see this matter through to the end that very night.

Initially, everything was brought into the open.

(While I only suggest this, I believe that I am pressing the real key to the psychology of world history into the reader's hand).

Faussecocheur was the only one who really mourned.

For the first time in his life, he deviated from his custom of regarding nothing on earth in a sentimental way. But this time the momentum of Weltschmerz cast a dark cloud over him, and the worm of sorrow gnawed at his soul.

"Marshal," he sighed, "it's such a terrible pity. Such a worthwhile young man! But you see, it's a natural law that idiots—who don't know what to do with it—are gifted with the greatest talent. What I could have achieved with the talent of this pathetic young man!

"I believe in the eternal laws of harmony. If you decrease the number of bankers, you increase the number of pickpockets. If you increase the number of senior teachers, madhouses become emptier. If you decrease the number of lyricists, you increase the number of conmen. The world is governed by the law of balanced equations.[135]

"Let us assume that young Liebrecht understood enough politics to set himself up like Dr. Steiner, or other contemporary directors of profundity, salvation, mysticism and human sexual development.[136] The people would have elected him Dalai Lama. Because the poor people need their Dalai Lamas. Where could they go otherwise, with their needs for faith and veneration? The skepticism of our age leaves no room for anything holy. Nothing is more timely than arrival of the Messiah. I await Him daily. Take, my dear Marshal, the case of Jesus Christ. I ask you, what would have happened to the Son of God if Paul hadn't established and disseminated His faith? I am a cleric. Why am I a cleric? Because I know that even God cannot do the slightest thing amongst humans without swindling. The church is necessary. God needs shamans, otherwise He loses prestige. Truth arises out of lies. Make me the Pope: it would be possible. But a Pope that was completely holy? Impossible! The poor young man has completely deceived himself. He has deceived himself by his own thoughts and actions. If only he had turned to me for help! But all his wonderful gifts went up in smoke. He lacked an understanding of politics. What should one do with such a young man? He *has to be* clubbed to death and then sanctified."

While the 8,000 European luminaries and their ladies are refreshing themselves in the vicinity of the Great Hall, let us find out about Jens Liebrecht's destiny.

What happened to him? Where was he?

He was now *seriously* ill. Six physicians percussed, auscultated, prodded, and swabbed. They all shook their heads seriously, and confirmed Schreck's adequate, immediate, and intuitive diagnosis.

A plump, white featherbed was set up in the library of the Great Hall. Jens Liebrecht was placed on it.

Warmed-up cooking lids were placed on his belly.

There he lay, in the midst of the spoiled waste of all sorts and conditions of happily secluded immortals. It wasn't that he lacked humanity. Everyone found him likeable. He had presented the world with a diverting play of an innocent who blows himself up. It had been a long time since mockers, bitter or joyful, had been sent to witness burnings at the stake. They only hurt themselves. Countess Perponcher sent wine jelly, *Geheimrätin* Prinzheimer cognac pralines. Two charmingly kinky peroxide blondes from the patriotic women's association "Zum schmerzhaften Mutterherzen"[137] helped with nursing. They took turns reading to him, to help him sleep. Material included Karl Marx's *Das Kapital* and Cry-Baby's great German coming-of-age and education novel *The Butterleeks, or The Demise of an Eminent Family.*[138]

The Grand Old Man was full of fatherly care. He turned to Schreck, the Berlin phenomenologist, on the balcony, saying "My dear Herr Professor, I congratulate you on your excellent talk. We must certainly do something for the unfortunate young man. How, in your opinion, should matters *proceed*?"

Schreck wisely put finger on nose, saying: "Well! It can and must only proceed in only one way. Generally, the *exitus lethalis* is the outcome. In any event, the man is genetically damaged. He might have inherited congenital paralysis from his father's side, or inherited neurological degeneration from his mother's side."

The grand old man thanked Schreck for the short but illuminating explanation, and took his leave.

At the same time, Foreign Minister Emil Blender betook himself to Faussecocheur, requesting a shirt, private conversation.

He said:

"*Herr Kollege*, I come to you with a discrete request. I am pleased to convey my government's thanks for your vigorous intervention, which prevented the unforeseeable consequences of revolution. I am sorry that the zig-zag politics of a mentally disordered man has so tragically impeded the progress of our state business. But I am still not sure whether we should fear more such incidents from him. In the long run, we cannot prevent the relationship between Herr Liebrecht and his constituents. Let us pose the following problem: Our unfortunate patient, who according to the doctors is genetically disabled, has—as you yourself have seen—already played with the idea of suicide. Let us suppose that the bomb which he carried around with him had blown him to bits. Or that he had fallen on the bayonets of your brave guard soldiers by accident. In retrospect, wouldn't that have been a *very good thing* for relationships of both our governments, and the extended progress of European consolidation?"

Faussecocheur looked understandingly into the minister's blue eyes

"My dear *Herr Kollege*," he said, "I understand that, as a patriot, you *must* think in this way. But let me respond as a patriot, with customary candor. With regard to *my own* patriotism, I must wish that *your own* patriotism is blessed as long and as often, with patriots like Herr Liebrecht. Patriots facilitate international business. As a patriot, I feel obliged to thank a fellow-patriot. Apart from that: if I could give you some political advice—never create martyrs. No other merchandise on earth even approximates the desirability of a martyr's wreath at a reduced price. Everyone wants to carry it, but no one wants to pay for it. It must therefore be made as expensive as possible to wear. Let them develop world history as organically as possible without violence, and leave everything further to the doctors and the press."

The hall filled up again.

An attendant sprinkled the stone floor with delicate eau de cologne.

Ladies winsomely waved their fans, and gentlemen smoked wispy cigarettes. Blue cigarette smoke wafted in delicate clouds over the dome of the mighty Great Hall. Like laughing goblins, lines and paragraphs of international; business floated high over the little blue clouds.

Satan had been driven out! The devil's expulsion was complete!

The fact that the maniacal attack of a mentally deranged man had threatened our entire *culture* now seemed an unbelievable nightmare. Everyone was in the pleasantest of spirits. Nerves were calmed, bodies soothed. Everywhere, the voice of *reason* was heard:

"Seventy-five per cent. No dividends. Bochum-Luxemburg Concern. American Petrol. Argentinian Beef Trust. Ehrlich-Hata shares no. 308.[139] Greenland Underground Limited of Austria. North American Solar Energy Utilities, fabulous appreciation."

Mannheimer resumed his seat at the telephone, spitting numbers into the receiver.

Marshal Boche de Trocadero, iron conqueror of Fatinitza, ceremoniously reopened the meeting. There he stood, resplendent in his masculine glory. He spoke powerfully and martially:

"I consider it Divine Providence that, during these consequential days, when Europe's fate hung in the balance, we have been in a position to show clearly who and what we are. Honored sirs, we have created world peace and harmony among men. We have saved Europe from world revolution. We have saved society and civilization. A man with hereditary mental disease, raised up by accident to power over Europe's brightest minds, threatened to blow up everyone, and with them *human civilization* itself. We want no thanks. We are satisfied with the consciousness that we have defended this beautiful country against mob rule. For the next 30 years we will faithfully remain on watch here. Yes, we swear it! We want to keep *protecting* this beautiful country from the mob and mob rule."

Thunderous applause from all sides. The marshal sat down proudly at the negotiation table.

Everyone was ready to think about business again.

Only a single soul in the hall was seized with dark discord—the awakened soul of the young Baldur Tünnes.

Peculiar! He still felt those dark, mournful eyes fixed upon him.

Hardly *human* at all.

There was something profoundly non-human about that man. A demon, an elemental being, foreign yet familiar.

What he had done was certainly nonpolitical and senseless. But don't we all have hours when we think that perhaps it's best to blow the whole damn thing up? That the entire human theater that we call life is nothing but lies, dreams, illusions?

What if the talents and facilities of this twisted, quixotic, ailing man had found a comfortable home and hearth? What if he could have developed *without* privation and repression? Could he not have developed into another Baldur Tünnes?

Baldur Tünnes let the images of this marvelous day roll by him like a movie film. The scene on the steps of the Great Hall, when the pale man jumped up, kissed him, and said: "Brother." The scene in the atrium, where he came up so trustingly, German to German. Those dark, mournful eyes. What eyes! Eyes of a Michelangelo, Eves of a wild, black jaguar. Where had he seen those eyes before?

Yes, he remembered now! They were his *father's* eyes.

Baldur went up to the grand old man.

"Papa," he said shyly, "please allow me to ask a question. Today you cared so nobly for the unhappy young man. They say that he is genetically damaged.

"You mentioned that you knew his father. You called him 'my loyal employee in one of my coal pits.' Did you perhaps know his mother as well?"

The grand old Tünnes, our region's patriarch, cast his eyes down and said thoughtfully:

"My God, Baldur, it was such a long time ago."

But, as every child in Germany knows, Baldur Tünnes possesses a great and noble soul.

He had to do something for the unhappy man.

He ascended the speaker's platform with a clear, pure surge of emotion and, with the faithful, blond tones of German "nature" that made him the nation's blue-eyed boy, said the following:

"Respected assembly. Before I finally come to more meritorious matters and begin the business side of our negotiations, allow me to draw your attention back to the tragicomedy of everything we have experienced, as if in a dream, during this memorable day.

"We have experienced with horror the short rise and rapid collapse of one of our fellow brothers.

"The doctors say that it is genetic.

"But far be it from us to adopt the Pharisee-like haughtiness, that says: Thank God, *I* am wiser than that. *Meine Herren*, we are *all*, and have been, patriots since our youth, and have done without the fame that we ought to have acquired.

"Let us not argue about it.

"In the name of my German National Party, I declare that we will undertake the cure and nursing costs of the labor leader and Communist Jens Liebrecht and, in case of his premature demise, funeral costs as well."

Like a malignant old she-monkey, little Mannheimer, that muse of world history, hopped up from his accustomed corner, where he was still spitting numbers into the telephone. No one could unravel his tangled thoughts, as his voice buzzed over everyone's head like a rasping shaving razor:

"Much better to pay the cure and funeral costs of your worthy party. Then you *too* will do something for the fatherland…"

Endnotes

1   Theodor Lessing, *Feind im Land. Satiren und Novellen* (Hannover: Wolf Albrecht Adam Verlag, 1923), 11–148; The Occupation of the Ruhr (*Ruhrbesetzung*) was a period of military occupation of the Ruhr region of Germany by France and Belgium between 11 January 1923 and 25 August 1925. France and Belgium occupied the heavily industrialized Ruhr Valley in response to Germany default-ing on reparation payments dictated by the Treaty of Versailles. Occupation worsened the German economic crisis, and German civilians engaged in acts of passive resistance. France and Belgium agreed to restructure Germany's payment of war reparations in 1924 and withdrew their troops from the Ruhr by August 1925. The Occupation of the Ruhr contributed to German re-armament and the growth of radical right-wing movements in Germany. Lessing comments acidly in this chapter on conditions at the start of the occupation.

2   More sarcasm: Regional West-Central German epithet for a fool. The most famous Tünnes is memorialized in Cologne. *Tünnes and Schäl* are figures from *Hänneschen-Theater*, the Cologne puppet theater. Lessing may also be referring to Hugo Stinnes (1870–1924).

3   *Boche* is a derogatory French word for German, "Fatinitza" is an operetta by Franz von Suppé (1819–1895). Lessing is sarcastically calling a fictitious French marshal a comic-opera general. Marshal of France is a French military distinc-tion (*titre de dignité*), rather than a military rank, that is awarded to generals for exceptional achievements.

4   More sarcasm. *Falsiloquus* (Latin) means lying. Thus, lying treaty (= Treaty of Versailles).

5   Baldr (also Balder, Baldur) is a god in Norse mythology and a son of the god Odin and the goddess Frigg. He has numerous brothers, such as Thor and Váli.

6   Lessing changes the name from *Falfiloques* to *Falsiloques*.

7   The German word *völkisch* is untranslatable. It denotes an exclusionary national-ity. Jews were not considered members of the *Volk*.

8   Probably a spoof on Karl Liebknecht (chapter 2 note 4)).

9   More sarcasm. The word *welthistorisch* was coined by Friedrich Hegel (1770–1831) for individuals who introduce world-impacting concepts and operate out-side the norms of civilization.

10   More sarcasm: *fausse* in French means false, and *cocheur* a wedge; Charles-Maurice de Talleyrand-Périgord (1754–1838), French politician and diplomat whose career spanned the regimes of Louis XVI, the years of the French Revolution, Napoleon, Louis XVIII, and Louis-Philippe.

11   Michelangelo Buonarroti (1475–1564), Florentine sculptor, painter, architect and poet of the High Renaissance who exerted a profound influence on the Western art.

12.   More sarcasm: Pupp von Kohlen. Pupp probably means Krupp, *Kohle*: coal.

13   Most probably Fritz Thyssen (1873–1951), German industrialist

14   *Vieux jeu.*

15   Possibly the banker Isaac Halberstein; Gewinner, international banker; Herr Plutussohn is lampooned in an issue of Maximilian Harden's periodical *Die Zukunft* as a plutocratic, insensitive glutton who demands only the finer things of life (*Die Zukunft*, vol. 4, 386, 392); probably Jay Gould (1836–1892), American financial speculator known for his sharp and often unscrupulous business practices; Maximilian Harden (Felix Ernst Witkowski)(1861–1927), influential German journalist and editor. Described at length in Theodor Lessing, *Der Jüdische Selbsthass* (Berlin: Jüdischer Verlag, 1930), 167–210; Theodor Lessing, *Jewish Self-Hate*, trans. and ed. by Peter C. Appelbaum and Benton Arnovitz (New York and Oxford: Berghahn Books, 2021), 115–140.

16   Joel 3:2 and 3:12: "Then I will enter into judgment with them there on behalf of my people and for My inheritance Israel, whom they have scattered among the nations and they have divided up My land." Also, "Let the nations be aroused. And come up to the Valley of Jehoshaphat, for there I will sit to judge all the nations on every side."

17   A sarcastic reference to the hall of mirrors in Versailles where the 1919 peace treaty was signed.

18   German civilization and culture (sometimes used derogatorily to suggest elements of racism, authoritarianism, or militarism).

19   William Shakespeare (1564–1616), widely regarded as the greatest writer in the English language and the world's greatest dramatist. A riff on *The Magic Mountain*, by Thomas Mann (1875–1955), which takes place in a luxury Swiss tuberculosis sanitarium.

20   *Wimmerlottchen* (original).

21 Thomas (1875–1955) and Heinrich (1871–1950) Mann, German novelist brothers. Both born in Lübeck. Throughout the novella, Thomas is *Männe* (Manny) Shakespeare and Heinrich is *Wimmerlottchen* or *Wimmerlotte* (Cry-Baby). As if on purpose, Lessing mixes the two up. Heinrich was the older brother and president of the fine poetry division of the Prussian Academy of Arts.

22 Pope Gregory I (c. 540 – 604), commonly known as Saint Gregory the Great, bishop of Rome from 3 September 590 to his death.

23 More sarcasm. Ernst Mach (1838–1916), Austrian physicist noted for his contribution to physics such as study of shock waves. The ratio of speed to that of sound is named the Mach number; Albert Einstein (1879–1955), German theoretical physicist who developed the seminal mass-energy equivalence formula $E=mc^2$ as well as the theory of general relativity.

24 *Volksgenossen(innen)*. Terms much used by the Nazis to exclude Jews and other undesirables.

25 More sarcasm. Until the Nazis destroyed it by expelling Jewish faculty members, the University of Göttingen was home to one of the world's preeminent mathematics departments.

26 Blue in German is both the color of the Imperial German Army uniform and an adjective used to describe inebriation,

27 More sarcasm. *Blender* means an imposter.

28 A targeted group of assassinations and wave of Roman Catholic violence against the Huguenots during the French Wars of Religion. Beginning the night of 23–24 August 1572, the massacre spread from Paris throughout France and killed 5,000–30,000 people.

29 A member of a class of serfs in ancient Sparta, intermediate in status between slaves and citizens.

30 *Costel* (*cultellus*), a medieval short sword.

31 The cooking pot.

32 Sepp Schwarbel. *Schwabbeln* means to blather.

33 More sarcasm: *Stach von Stachelbart*. A *Stachelbart* is a mushroom of the genus *Hericium*.

34   *Genossen.*

35   Allusion to the words of the Kaiser when he announced the *Burgfrieden* (civil truce) on 2 August, 1914.

36   The Gordian knot is a legend of Phrygian Gordium associated with Alexander the Great. It is often used as a metaphor for an intractable problem solved by finding a different approach to it ("cutting the Gordian knot"): When confronted with it, Alexander did not try to unravel the Gordian knot—he, cut it through.

37   French colonial troops from North Africa and Senegal were much disliked, and accused of murder of German civilians.

38   Strange sentiments from a Jew.

39   *Klage, Anklage.*

40   The Spartacus League was a left-wing Marxist revolutionary movement in Germany during and just after World War I.

41   *Habebald.*

42   More sarcasm: unbaptized Jews were rarely raised to the nobility in Germany. The opprobrious term given for Jewish/Yiddish-accented German was *jüdeln* or *mauscheln.*

43   *Nationale Volkspartei.*

44   *Volksgenossen.*

45   An opprobrious Hebrew/Arabic epithet for unbelievers, people who belong nowhere.

46   The law of parallelogram of forces states that if two vectors acting on a particle at the same time be represented in magnitude and direction by the two adjacent sides of a parallelogram drawn from a point their resultant vector is represented in magnitude and direction by the diagonal of the parallelogram drawn from that point. More sarcasm: this has nothing to do with the narrative.

47   German civilization and culture (sometimes used derogatorily to suggest elements of racism, authoritarianism, or militarism).

48   *Staat* und *Volk.*

49   During the war years, Thomas Mann took political and aesthetic positions that were diametrically opposed to those of his brother Heinrich. From the beginning, Thomas Mann justified, praised and celebrated the war, and repeatedly focused on the special condition of the German psyche which, in his view, explained the German readiness for war as well as his own intellectual background.

50   *Sein* and *Sosein*.

51   Sigmund Freud (1856–1939), Austrian neurologist and founder of psychoanalysis.

52   Women in Phrygia (a bronze age a kingdom in the west central part of Anatolia, in what is now Asian Turkey) served as priestesses.

53   Tomi, Männe Shakespeare = Thomas Mann the Younger. The *elder* Mann (Thomas Johann Heinrich Mann) was a grain merchant and senator in Lübeck. The ladies with hatpins have understood Tomi's subtle critique of the philistine bourgeoisie (including by implication the *Getreidebaron und Senator Thomas Johann Heinrich Mann*) and are prepared to attack him, Tomi, as a result. They shout a warning that he, Tomi, should prepare to defend himself for making such vicious remarks.

54   *Volk*.

55   *Geist* and *Seele*.

56   *Gemeinschaft* (community) versus *Gesellschaft* (society)

57   *Gangeshofer*: a disparaging German nickname for Rabindranath Tagore (1861–1941), Indian polymath, poet, musician, artist and Ayurveda-researcher. The Darmstadt self-seeker refers to Hermann Graf von Keyserling (1880–1946), Baltic German philosopher and founder of the *Gesellschaft für Freie Philosophie* (Society for Free Philosophy) in Darmstadt. The mission of this school was to bring about the intellectual reorientation of Germany.

58   *Späneschnitzler*

59   Friedrich Hegel (1770–1831), German philosopher and important figure in German idealism.

60   In his Botanical Writings (1790), the great writer, poet and scientist Johann Wolfgang von Goethe (1749–1832) was the first to use the term morphology.

61   Cecil Rhodes (1853–1902), British businessman, statesman, imperialist, mining magnate, and politician in Southern Africa who served as Prime Minister of the Cape Colony from 1890 to 1896. The damage from his noxious colonial policy remains with us.

62   Satirical German-language magazine first published in Berlin on 7 May 1848, and appearing "daily, except for weekdays."

63   Light cavalry regiments of the French army recruited primarily from the indigenous populations of Algeria, Tunisia and Morocco, much disliked by Germans.

64   Jean-Jacques Rousseau (1712–1778), Genevan philosopher, writer and composer whose political philosophy influenced the progress of European Enlightenment.

65   *Gesicht* (face), *Antlitz* (countenance).

66   Peer Gynt is a five act play in verse by Henrik Ibsen (1828–1906) which blends poetry with social satire and realistic scenes with surreal ones. Wilhelm II was often described as the *Reisekaiser* (traveling Kaiser) because of his propensity to travel all the world.

67   The Papal Nuncio in Germany during the 1920s was future Pope Pius XII Eugenio Pacelli (1876–1958). Francesco Nitti (1868–1953), Italian statesman who was Prime Minister during 1919, but ousted by Mussolini in 1920, Nitti held strong anti-fascist views. The reason for Lessing using this name is unclear.

68   The Erfurt Program, adopted by the Social Democratic Party of Germany during the Congress at Erfurt in 1891, declared the imminent death of capitalism and necessity of socialist ownership of means of production. The Party intended to pursue these goals by legal political participation rather than revolution.

69   *Schmuser* (original).

70   *Völkisch-National.*

71   The *Ephebi* were young Greeks who left their families and underwent a period of military training. If they passed muster, they took an oath to serve the city, were given a spear, shield, cloak and hat, and set out to guard the frontier.

72   Confused mythological references. The *Oresteia* by Aeschylus (c. 525–524-456/455 BCE) takes place after the death of Oedipus. Oedipus correctly solves the riddle of the Sphinx, who then becomes so angry and frustrated that she leaps to her death from the Theban Acropolis. At the conclusion of *Oedipus at*

Colonnus by Sophocles (c. 497/496–406/405 BCE), the hero throws himself off a cliff in that city.

73 *Volksbegeisterung.*

74 Lessing is speaking of the 1918–1919 influenza pandemic, which infected one third of the world's population and killed at least 50 million.

75 In mythology the phoenix was associated with Egyptian sun worship. When a phoenix (lifespan c. 500 years) sensed that its end was near, it built a pyre of aromatic wood and burned itself alive. From the ashes a new phoenix arose, gathered the ashes, enclosed them in an egg of myrrh and flew off with the egg to Heliopolis, where it deposited it on the altar in the Temple of Ra. In Egyptian mythology, Ra was the incorporation of the *Sonnenseele* (original).

76 Corybants were members of a sect of Cybele worshipers known for crested costumes and wild dancing in honor of the goddess.

77 *Sein.*

78 A major Nietzschean concept.

79 A derisive allusion to the classic work by that name by Friedrich Nietzsche (1844–1900), seminal nineteenth century thinker whose philosophy asserted the Übermensch and the will to power.

80 Alfred Kerr (Kempner) (1867–1948), influential German theater critic and essayist of Jewish descent, nicknamed the *Kulturpapst* (Culture Pope); George Bernard Shaw (1856–1950), Irish playwright, critic, polemicist and political activist; Carl Sternheim (William Carl Franke, 1878–1942), German playwright and short story writer of Jewish descent.

81 In Wagner's *Die Walküre*, Siegmund and Sieglinde are identical Wälsung twins who fall in love, mate, and produce *Siegfried.*

82 Yggdrasil (from Old Norse Yggdrasill) is an immense mythical tree that plays a central role in Norse cosmology, where it connects the Nine Worlds.

83 The *Neue Rundschau*, formerly *Die neue deutsche Rundschau* is a quarterly German literary magazine founded in 1890. With over 130 years of continuous history, it is one of the oldest cultural publications in Europe, and was one of the most important forums for literature and essay writing in the Wilhelmine Era and Weimar Republic.

84 Yiddish: A person regarded as weak-willed or timid.

85 Dadaism was an art movement of the European avant-garde in the early twentieth century, developed in reaction to World War I. The Dada movement consisted of artists who rejected the logic, reason, and aestheticism of modern capitalist society, instead expressing nonsense, irrationality, and anti-bourgeois protest in their works.

86 This is Shakespeare's genius. He deliberately leaves this issue open to eternal question. As Polonius says: "Mad call I it, for, to define true madness, what is't but to be nothing else but mad? (*Hamlet*, Act 2 Scene 2).

87 Untranslatable wordplay: *Sinn* (sense), *Unsinn* (nonsense), *Wahnsinn* (madness).

88 *Mutmensch, Tatmensch.*

89 Again, *Sinn* versus *Unsinn.*

90 Untranslatable wordplay of *Leben, lebendig, lebig, lebevoll.*

91 Daniel 5:6.

92 A mixture of powdered soap, camphor oil of rosemary, alcohol, and water invented, or at least named, by the German Renaissance physician Paracelsus (1493/1494–1541) in the 1500s.

93 Numbers 22:21–39. Balak, king of Moab sends Balaam, son of Beor, to curse Israel. Balaam sends word that he can only do what God commands, and God has, through a dream, told him not to go. Balak sends higher-ranking priests and offers Balaam honors; Balaam continues to press God and God finally permits him to go, but with instructions to say only what he commands. Balaam sets out in the morning with the princes of Moab. God becomes angry, and sends the Angel of the Lord to prevent him. At first, the Angel is seen only by the donkey Balaam is riding, which tries to avoid the angel. After Balaam starts beating the donkey for refusing to move, it is miraculously given the power to speak to Balaam. and complains about Balaam's treatment. Balaam is now allowed to see the Angel, who informs him that the donkey's turning away from the messenger is the only reason the Angel did not kill him. Balaam immediately repents, but is told to go on. When he sees the Children of Israel, he blesses instead of cursing them ("How goodly are your tents, O Jacob, your dwelling-places, O Israel").

94 *Männe* (original). The plural of *Mann* (Man) is *Männer.*

95 *Reichsoberhaupt.* More sarcasm. The German Empire ceased to exist after World War I.

96 Dionysus is the Greek god of the grape-harvest, winemaking and wine, of fertility, ritual madness, religious ecstasy, festivity and theater.

97 UFA GmbH is a German film and television production. Its history comes from *Universum Film AG* (abbreviated in logo as *UFA*), which was a major German film company headquartered in Babelsberg, producing and distributing motion pictures from 1917 through to the end of the Nazi era. By 1923 it had produced major movies such a "Nosferatu" (F.W. Murnau) and "Dr. Mabuse the Gambler" (Fritz Lang).

98 Walter Bloem (1898-presumed dead 1945), German writer known under the pseudonym Kilian Koll. When World War I began, Bloem volunteered for service at age sixteen, was wounded several times, and highly decorated.

99 In Greek mythology, Kleio (Clio) was the muse of history.

100 In Marxist philosophy, the dictatorship of the proletariat is a state of affairs in which a proletarian party holds political power. The socialist revolutionary Joseph Weydemeyer (1818–1866) coined the term "dictatorship of the proletariat," which Karl Marx (1818–1883) and Friedrich Engels (1820–1895) adopted to their philosophy and economics.

101 *Meyers Konversations-Lexikon* or *Meyers Lexikon* was a major encyclopedia in the German language that existed in various editions, and by several titles, from 1839 to 1984, when it merged with the *Brockhaus Enzyklopädie.*

102 Friedrich Gundolf, born Friedrich Leopold Gundelfinger (1880–1931), German-Jewish literary scholar and poet and one of the best known academics of the Weimar Republic.

103 In Greek mythology, maenads were the female followers of Dionysus and the most significant members of the Thiasus, the god›s retinue

104 The National Constituent Assembly, acting on the night of 4 August 1789, announced, "The National Assembly abolishes the feudal system entirely." It abolished the seigneurial rights of the Second Estate (nobility) and tithes gathered by the First Estate (the Catholic clergy). On 4 August 1914, Great Britain declared war on Germany after German Invasion of Belgium.

105 More sarcasm: It was extremely difficult for an unconverted Jew to be ennobled in Germany.

106 *Anforderungen, Forderungen.*

107 Balduin Bählamm was a creation of the cartoonist and poet Wilhelm Busch (1832–1908). He is the symbol of the frustrated poet who is never taken seriously.

108 *Fressen.*

109 Erich Marcks (1861–1938), historian whose career spanned the *Kaiserreich* through the Third Reich

110 Ariadne was a Cretan princess in Greek mythology mostly associated with mazes and labyrinths because of her involvement in the myths of the Minotaur and Theseus.

111 The Battle of Waterloo (18 June 1815); Arthur Wellesley First Duke of Wellington (1769–1852); Gebhard von Blücher (1742–1819). The banker Nathan Mayer Rothschild (1777–1836) financed the British. In the nineteenth century an anti-semitic story arose that accused him of having used his early knowledge of victory at the Battle of Waterloo to speculate on the stock exchange and make a fortune. The story is untrue.

112 Luxury Berlin hotels.

113 Leopold von Ranke (1795–1886), German historian and founder of modern source-based history; Heinrich von Treitschke (1834–1896), German historian, political writer, antisemite. Ranke's goal of *wie es eigentlich gewesen ist* is an impossible one. Theodor Lessing, *Geschichte als Sinngebung des Sinnlosen.* (Munich: C.H. Beck, 1921).

114 Count Otto von Bismarck (1815–1898), conservative German statesman who masterminded the unification of Germany in 1871 and served as its first chancellor until 1890; Friedrich von Holstein, *The Holstein Diaries*, vol. 2, edited by Norman Rich and M.H. Fischer (Cambridge: Cambridge University Press, 1957), xv.

115 *Vaterländische Volkspartei.*

116 *Alle Menschen werden Brüder*, From "An die Freude" by Friedrich von Schiller (1759–1805).

117 After Matthew 5:17.

118 *Mäkler und Mächler.*

119 The Buddha (also known as Siddhattha Gotama or Siddhārtha Gautama) philosopher, mendicant, meditator, spiritual teacher, and religious leader who lived in Ancient India (c. 5th to 4th century BCE); St. Francis of Assisi (1181/82–1226), Italian Catholic friar, deacon, philosopher, mystic and preacher.

120 *Wichtig* and *nichtig*.

121 "Der Spiegelmensch" is part of a trilogy published by AustroBohemian novelist, playwright and poet Franz Werfel (1890–1945) in 1920. Thamal, a Faust-like figure, tires of the contemplative life and seeks peace in a monastery.

122 *Erlauchten* und *Erleuchteten*.

123 See Goethe's "Der Zauberlehrling." (*The Sorcerer's Apprentice*), *Die ich rief, die Geister/Werd ich nun nicht los!* (The spirits that I called up/I now cannot get rid of!).

124 Max Stirner (Johann Kaspar Schmidt) (1806–1856), German philosopher often seen as one of the forerunners of nihilism, existentialism, psychoanalytic theory, postmodernism and individualist anarchism; Mikhail Alexandrovich Bakunin (1814–1876),Russian revolutionary anarchist.

125 *Mittun, mittuten*.

126 Original: *Schauerl*.

127 Raphael: *Die Sonne tönt nach alter Weise/In Brudersphären Wettgesang.* Goethe's *Faust I*, "Prolog im Himmel," lines 1–2.

128 Untranslatable wordplay. Theodor Adorno (1903–1969) used three German terms to describe objectivity: *Objektivität, Sachlichkeit, Gegenständlichkeit*. Lessing uses the first two: *Objektivität*: The *objektiver Geist* (objective spirit) as set out by Hegel; *Sachlichkeit*: delusion of objectivity, matter-of-factness and detachment that denies and represses the subjectivity inherent in the objective. *Die neue Sachlichkeit* (the new objectivity) was a movement in German art that arose during the 1920s as a reaction against expressionism

129 *Volksgenossen, Landeskinder*.

130 Anatole France (born François-Anatole Thibault) (1844–1924), French poet, journalist, and novelist; Lessing is making fun of a Catholic priest with the names Amandus (loving) and Polygamios (polygamous). Cologne is Germany's largest Catholic archdiocese.

131   Raymond Poincaré (1860–1934) served as president of France from (1913–1920), noted for his strongly anti-German attitudes.; *Maurenbrecher* (original): Moorbreaker; David Lloyd George (1863–1945), British statesman and British Prime Minister from 1916 to 1922; Thomas Woodrow Wilson (1856–1924), American politician, lawyer, and academic who served as the twenty-eighth president of the United States from 1913 to 1921. By 1923, Wilson had been incapacitated by a stroke for 3 years. Lloyd George and Wilson played leading roles in drawing up the Versailles Treaty; Hellmut von Gerlach (1866–1935), German journalist and politician.

132   More sarcasm: *Renitenz* (defiance) instead of *Resistenz* (resistance).

133   *Geld* (money); *gelten*: to count.

134   *Edel sei der Mensch/hilfreich und gut*, from "das Göttliche," by Goethe.

135   Every chemical equation adheres to the law of conservation of mass (Antoine Lavoisier, 1743–1794, postulated in 1789), which states that matter cannot be created or destroyed

136   Rudolf Steiner (1861–1925) Austrian philosopher, social reformer, architect, esotericist, and claimed clairvoyant.

137   At the aching mother's heart.

138   Lessing is referring to *Buddenbrooks*, written by Thomas, not Heinrich Mann.

139   Paul Ehrlich (1854–1915), Nobel prize-winning German physician and scientist who worked in the fields of hematology, immunology, and antimicrobial chemotherapy; Sahachiro Hata (1873–1938) who assisted in developing arsphenamine (salvarsan) for treatment of syphilis in 1909 in the laboratory of Paul Ehrlich.

4

Comrade Levi, 1914/15[1]

When the Great European War began, 26-year-old Siegfried Levi, scion of a second-hand trader from Hanover, consulted several military physicians, in an effort to obtain exemption from military service. However, against his expectations, they declared him perfectly fit, with no prospect of dispensation for a reservist with no prior service.

Levi decided that immediate enlistment as a volunteer would secure better conditions than mandatory conscription after a long, anxious wait. After innumerable failed applications, he was accepted through a ruse. It became apparent that the first company of number I replacement battalion of the 124th regiment of the line was only recruiting fifty volunteers. Although he arrived in the regimental barracks courtyard two hours before time, stairs, passages and doors of the large building were already occupied by at least 300 young men, each of whom hoped that only *he* would be honored with the Emperor's uniform. Levi didn't even try to join the throng on the steps leading to the mustering hall, but remained in the empty courtyard. He noticed a ladder leaning against one of the open upper floor windows, and climbed up into a suitable barracks room corner. He hid in one of the third floor cubicles until the appointed time, tiptoed to the colonel's room, and was first in line before the exemption commission. In answer to the amazed colonel's question what *he* was doing there, Levi at once called out in a clear and passionate voice: "To die for the fatherland, of course!". The amazed officers looked at him with misgiving; however, in view of his certification of a clean bill of health, they registered him into the regiment.

Thus, Levi became a soldier. Until now, he had owned the Burgstraße store inherited from his father and grandfather. As thanks for his business acumen, the store had become known throughout the town as a 'salon d'antiquités.' After the war began, it received a new company nameplate, and was renowned as the *Deutches Haus für Altertümer* [German House of Antiquities]. Newly enlisted bright eyed and bushy tailed into the Great War, he looked like a rare, delicate, dusty antique from the distant past amongst the fair haired, enthusiastic North German youth. His bearing lacked martial correctness and he slouched while walking. His ever anxious, faded face reflected the moody apathy of centuries which left nothing to the imagination. His legs were so incurably bandy that all commissioned and non-commissioned drill officers picked barrack yard blossoms from in between them. Heavy artillery pieces were aimed through his legs, which represented a gap in the front through which the wicked French could one day drive into our German fatherland. Levi accepted these and other jokes with unflappable equanimity, even making quips about his legs at his own expense, laughing wistfully, inasmuch as cheerful laughter could find a home in his hand-me-down face. Only rarely was he seen laughing.

During two months of basic training he did exactly what he was commanded, not a scrap more. He detested all unnecessary movement, and consistently entertained the sergeant with evidence that today excused him from horizontal bar exercises because of "pain in the back of the knee," tomorrow from drill because of a "finger infection." He acquired the company name of "the great slacker," together with our general contempt. The rest of us were young and cheerful, loaded as if by an electrical charge with equal measures of enthusiasm and rage, ready in the exuberant energy of the moment for an excursion into the heady heights of courage. Comrade Levi had the effect of a leaden weight on outstretched wings. Was it therefore surprising, that we all avoided him like the plague? Lieutenant von Lieven used to say: "his face spoils all my enjoyment of war," and someone went so far as to secretly swear that this "battle mocker" would not live long. Warrant officer Kracht, a blond Germanic giant of sterling qualities who went under the byname "King of the Germans," couldn't bear to see or even sniff the ludicrous soldier and said calmly to his comrades: "I'll send him on patrol, freeing the German army of a useless mouth."

Four weeks later, we decamped. It was the week of 27 September.

Transported in many thousands, we were informed of our destination in the train carriage: Not, as we thought, to the fight against France, but to Northern Belgium where, after the occupation of Brussels and Ghent, a fierce battle for Antwerp and he North Sea coast would have to be fought. During the endless journey, during which we stopped for hours at smaller stations until we arrived in Aachen after 4 hours, Levi sat in shirt sleeves in a corner of the cattle car, dispensing strategic information. His knowledge of military detail was extraordinary. When asked about the current location of a specific regiment, he knew not only all its details, but the names of its leaders, promotion histories of Kluck, Hindenburg and Emmich, ranking lists of von Bülow and von Moltke,[2] and everyone's personal and family relationships, marriage and inheritance details. Each one of these was compartmentalized in his mind. Who else would have cared about such things? Nobody! The young Lieutenant von Lieven, who was traveling with us, exclaimed repeatedly: "The devil! How does he know all these things?" Levi, meanwhile, squatted quietly in his corner, drawing genealogical contours in the air with his pencil, explaining that the Lievens and the Liefens were of different origins: The original Captain von Lieven from Stargard[3] and Major Liefen from Königsberg[4] couldn't possibly be related, and the lieutenant's family was related to the princely family which, a hundred years earlier, was originally called Levi but ennobled after conversion. The little lieutenant, overwhelmed by evidence of his Jewish origins, began to find the omniscient Levi "scary." He said shudderingly that, instead of a field Bible. Levi carried a shot-through army list full of penciled notes in his knapsack.

After disembarkation, our terrible march towards the enemy began. Every day we waited for the great beginning of our "baptism by fire." I remained near Levi on purpose: not only because he interested me, but because being near him brought me relief from the weary march. Firstly, he had the habit of continuously mumbling opera and operetta melodies, by whose rhythm he slouched forward on the march, just as he did in the barracks courtyard. "Sirs," he said "every living creature has its own cadence, by which it moves most easily. Each person must test his own rhythm. As for me, I currently prefer the melody 'Dearest mother, please don't die' and 'I have a rendezvous at six, with Erika, my dear, sweet hussy.' Some melodies ring my chimes better than others." This mechanical slouching to the beat of a melody, repeated a thousand times, seemed to preserve his strength.

Even today, when I hear one opera melody or other, the image of my whimsical comrade appears before me, slouching forward with sober imperturbability and objective disenchantment over the long swampy or frozen highway, sucking an endless supply of gumdrops, which he shared generously with his comrades. "I imported large batches of these hard gumdrops from America immediately after war was declared, because I didn't know how long they would remain available. We don't manufacture anything similar in Germany. American gumdrops can't be swallowed whole, and must be sucked for many hours before they start to dissolve. In this way, gums remain moist on the march, which is not the case with the stuff that others chew. Many smoke cigarettes while marching: they'll rue the day, because smoking prematurely destroys the bronchial and alveolar lining.[5] Some of you carry kola lozenges with you, others carry sugar. Both are dangerous, because they dissolve in a few seconds, releasing poison into the system."[6] Warrant Officer Kracht sensibly carries dried plums with him. His plums are of the Catharine variety. Sultana plums are better, but the best plums of all—King plums—come from the vicinity of Tours, France. The handiest plums are the Bismarck variety: they contain no dust at all from the main Berlin causeway, and can be chewed in dried form for hours on end; even the pit leaves a pleasant bitter almond aftertaste. By contrast, comrade Bokelberg has been swindled into wasting good money on Hirth's Electric Regeneration Lozenges, and Lieutenant von Lieven chews pralines, thereby ruining his teeth, which already have several fillings. All these are poison, but American gumdrops, taken no more than twice a day, are the answer." Very soon Levi's American gumdrops became company favorites. There was always someone asking: "Well, Levi, d'you have another gumdrop?" whereupon Levi scooped out a large amount of sticky drops from his bottomless trousers pocket.

The next day, Levi's usefulness shone in a new and more brilliant light. It occurred in a large stable, where we overnighted in the straw. We had joined up that afternoon with parts of the regiment coming from another direction in a town (if I'm not mistaken) called Nachtigall. The staff, led by our colonel, quartered in a farmhouse near our stable, and the muffled sound of faraway artillery could be heard in the distance. The old colonel shambled out of the farmhouse in which he spent the night, entered the stable, and suddenly disappeared into the mist on the other side. Before this happened, we noticed that the regimental adjutant had come in several times to ask the enlisted men lying there for newspapers. The goodhearted young men unthinkingly gave him all the reading material they had, until not a single additional printed page could be scared up. Around 11.00 p.m., while the men were sleeping, the adjutant arrived yet again with his lantern to beg, borrow or steal even more reading material. None were left, and he departed ranting and raving.

Immediately afterwards, a high-ranking officer appeared, walking (or trying to walk) unsteadily, trying to disturb no one, between the rows of horses while we lay in the straw. It was our colonel, whom we called "the old man," lantern in hand, scurrying half bent over out of the stable into the field. Suddenly Levi appeared, bowed, and discreetly handed him a package of well folded best quality toilet paper. The crabby colonel accepted the package, glancing over the meek, submissive figure standing before him, slouching unpleasantly. Suddenly seeing the humor in all this, he clapped Levi on the shoulder: "What's your name?" "Siegfried Levi," he replied. The colonel wanted to walk right past him, cutting short the painful interview, but Levi doggedly remained at his side, using the opportunity to confront him with some well-chosen words. "Herr *Oberst*," he began, "the vehicle with the general staff maps."—"Now is not the time!" Levi continued undeterred: "The vehicle with the general staff maps must be serviced by a man who understands maps, charts and standard reference works, and knows how to organize all the literature that accompanies the regiment." "Why should *you* care?" the colonel interrupted, on one hand in an effort to get rid of the annoying man, on the other out of a sense of obligation for his well-mannered speaking manner and welcome gift. "Go speak to your immediate superior about this." "Who is he?" "Sergeant Kracht. Now stop bothering me," the Colonel commanded brusquely. "That is his responsibility!" But Levi, who didn't have a disciplined bone in his body, replied familiarly: "So can I refer him to you in this matter, Herr *Oberst*?" The colonel became angry: "Dismiss!" he roared. Levi shuffled back into the straw.

"Damn it," I said, "how could you say something like that? You've torn it now; the colonel is furious." Levi shook his little rascally head, as if weighing both sides of the issue. "His impression of this little encounter will remain." "How?" I whispered back, so as not to disturb our comrades, half-asleep in the straw in the evening twilight. "The colonel won't look at me again without thinking about it." We both fell asleep. Next morning, Levi reported to the "King of the Germans," saying that the colonel had ordered him to report to his immediate superior for the position of map coordinator. Only the colonel could fill such a position, so Kracht knew nothing about it. He wouldn't even have thought of troubling himself about the "company eyesore" had the colonel not waved to him occasionally from his horse while on the march, asking whether he had a man named Levi in his company, and whether he qualified for "topographic duty." Kracht, who had no idea what the word "topographic" meant, sensed that Levi's star was somehow in the ascendant, and began to talk about his scholarliness. Lieutenant von Lieven, who couldn't escape the thought that his name really was Levi, warmly confirmed this. When the elderly Colonel von Krosigk's gaze fell upon Levi's slouching figure singing "Dearest mother, please don't die," he thought of last night's painful episode, and gave Levi the sought-after position. A better "intellectual sutler" could not have been found. He completely reorganized all reference material according to a simplified system that he had devised. In this way, every available chart, map, and reference work was easily available on every type of demand.

Now began the terrible days when the very air we breathed was one solid mass of finely powdered, molten lead through which we were remorselessly driven forward like a herd of half blind half crazed animals, seeing nothing but blood, blood, even more blood. Our ears were filled with screams of pain and madness which filled the heavens. I feel it my duty to report on our many glorious deaths, and would not dare desecrate the unspeakable by thoughtless comments about our tragicomic comrade. However, memories of the past months are so fraught with grisly images that I would rather lighten my soul by recording more harmless images of musketeer Levi. Who would have expected the miraculous fraternization between Levi and the "King of the Germans?" Kracht the Hun, the handsomest man I ever saw compared to the revolting caricature of Comrade Levi, was in his element as soon as the bashing up began, but helpless against ordinary daily chores. The man who killed the dragon[7] was helpless against a gnat, and Levi used this to good effect. It became clear that, whenever we wanted anything from Kracht, we had to go through Levi. This was the case even with Lieven.

It all began with a matter of army boots, soon after the first night battle. The first fall frost prevented men from putting their boots on again after they had taken them off for the night. Many suffered so badly from the pressure of boot leather that they couldn't resist the temptation to take them off their swollen feet in the evening. They knew that, as soon as the command came to march off, the expansion of their warmed up feet and contraction of the leather would prevent them from putting their boots on again. Levi produced a bottle of collodion with which he painted over the men's toes, producing a varnish which lessened the pain of boot pressure. However, the putting on of boots on a cold winter morning remained a torture. He came up with a simple remedy. He stuffed the frozen boots with straw and newspaper, set them alight, and as soon as they caught fire the men plunged their feet into the flames and stamped them out. The boots then fitted like a glove, and the warmth was welcome as well.

The highlight—if you could call it that—of our comrades' war experiences came with the attack on Chaudfontaine[8] Castle, which belonged to a Belgian nobleman. Shots were deceitfully fired from its basement windows and skylights on our unsuspecting, apparently well-received German soldiers. In response, a detachment in which both Levi and I served was ordered to ruthlessly clean out the areas of the old building occupied by *francs tireurs*.[9] Our rightfully embittered troops took the opportunity to drag out every sack, box and crate that was not nailed down, in the hope of sending their contents back home to wives or parents from the nearest rest stop. But the overall discipline of our troops was impeccable, and all such individual "requisitioning" of valu-ables from the castle was severely punished. Everything that couldn't simply be thrown away on subsequent difficult marches was faithfully returned to its original owner. It was amusing and instructive to observe how, during storming of the castle, everyone tried to take an individual souvenir. Despite the weight of a forty-pound knapsack, each soldier burdened himself with useless objects, which he regarded as valuable and worth taking home.

In the middle of this wild, greedy melee, Levi calmly slouched through the castle halls singing the song about his please-don't die-mother. Here and there he stopped, gazing appreciatively at an old painting, admiringly inspecting bronzes, ancestral portraits and gobelin tapestries. He was the only one who understood anything about the significance of these objets d'art, and explained their significance to us without any hint of greed or desire to take anything away. This only changed when he entered a side apartment and spotted a small sowing table: he rushed up to it, and with a joyous howl took some things out of its drawers which disappeared forthwith into his trousers pockets. The items turned out to be a roll of black and one of white twine, a large supply of pins and trousers buttons, and a pair of scissors. This constituted all his Chaudfontane war plunder. He was the only one to easily take and keep his booty, which was the only positive, useful contribution from the proud storming of Chaudfontaine...

Through these small services, the black sheep of the regiment compensated for his uselessness in gun battles and hand to hand combat. I never saw him take an objective without becoming disturbed. When we lay side by side in a trench and saw a far-off Englishman fall, we joked about it to Levi, saying: "*You* are the one who killed him." He became pale as a sheet, and for days after kept confirming that I must have made a mistake—*he* could *never* have killed that Englishman.

Before I relate how this all ended, I must consider an event that reminded me of the intuitive nature of a sober man, in contrast to orders by thoughtless idiots. November 10 brought with it the bloodiest fighting that I can recall. We had dug ourselves into the frosty earth when the general's order came to assault and take a nearby town occupied by the British and French, but mainly the British, by morning. This order was couched in a so devil-may-care a way that Colonel von Krosigk—who rightly judged the danger of storming a camp adjacent to a forest with insufficient artillery cover—tore out his remaining scanty locks. The problem was that our heavy cannon would only be in place the next morning, far too late to be of any use. The general had designated the town of Grootschoote[10] as rendezvous point, without saying a word about the fact that it was still in enemy hands. His command was crystal clear. Through our binoculars, we saw with amazement great structures, behind which machine guns had been brought up, emerging in the fiery night glow like colossal clay pyramids, such as I had never seen before. Both our companies were directed to take part in the attack. Our regimental officers were comforted by the fact the Goslar sharpshooters had occupied our earlier quarters 15 minutes from our trenches. But they were so exhausted from nine days of ceaseless battle that they could not be relied on for the attack on Grootschoote imposed from higher up.

The undertaking proved more complicated than the general had thought. We succeeded in massing troops together around the town from three sides and attacking during the night. But it soon became clear that the enemy, sheltering under the starlight protection of the eerie, towering pyramids, had salvaged the ordinance park and gathered behind the forest. Terrible street fighting with frantic inhabitants forced our soldiers to attack each individual house, while the British ruthlessly destroyed the town in which they had previously quartered. The cry of cattle tortured in the flames; terror of tied up horses; wail of dogs through the night air; crack of beams about to collapse; black clouds over a meager moon; a harsh east wind that quickly drove the fire into grain silos and straw piles, roofs and beams; the burning church; the thousand-year-old church tower collapsing suddenly into the demented night as if struck by one massive blow; voices around me from every possible direction and source. Everything merged into a Dantesque vision from hell.

It all appears to me now like a chaotic sensation, so lunatic and senseless that the mad world appeared to have collapsed into hell fire. In the streets between the burning houses, corpses were strewn so thickly that advancing troops had only to use their bayonets like a jumping pole stuck into the heap of dead animals and men, to get over piled up obstacles Our patrol reported powerful enemy artillery forces a short distance away, behind the woods. We waited hourly for arrival of our heavy guns, but they came too late to protect us from hails of British shells and shrapnel from their sheltered positions. Our occupation of Grootschoote didn't help us much.

Captain Krüger, a calm and thoughtful man who avoided unnecessary wastage of men's lives, would have preferred to return to our previous position, but the general ordered "Hold the town until our cannons arrive." A chain of thirty men maintained the rear link with the Goslarers at the Montjoie feudal estate, with a man every 50 meters, and the wish was relayed as if telegraphically across the chain: "Come already!" Although our men crawled on their stomachs like snakes through the freshly ploughed fields, they couldn't carry on without any kind of protection, and the air was a flaming cauldron.

At the crossroads of two highways, a black, tarred barrack stood on a small escarpment in the middle of the field. The colonel decided to make this his center of operations. When we attacked the house, however, we found, piled up to the ceiling, over 300 seriously wounded English and French soldiers, who had been left in the lurch during their comrades' headlong withdrawal. Gruesomely penned up together in an asphyxiating atmosphere of suppuration and sweaty fever, their only recourse lay in one pale, helpless junior physician and two exhausted medical orderlies. No sooner did this hell of human misery fall into our hands, than the colonel recklessly ordered that they be carried outside. In this way the barracks, which were not shot at from the woods, could be used for our staff or our own wounded. Hardly had the clearing-up operations of the whimpering, babbling half-dead soldiers begun, than a huge shell completely tore off the roof of the hideous house. A sea of dust from the beams and splinters poured down over friend and foe alike. Each tried to save himself from the wreckage, and in the new chaos upon chaos, all commands faded away. Everyone waited upon the sharpshooters. After message after message had been dispatched. Levi and I volunteered as orderlies, to urge the colonel to order the Goslarers to attack the forest, now named *le forêt d'août*.

The answer came: "Hang on for another hour, until the Goslarers are near enough to attack." We almost wept from frustration. The sharpshooter officers cursed the colonel for not having enough guts to expose the tired out troops on our behalf. The attack had taken place too soon, we must retreat to our old positions, and attack again the next morning. Reasonable suggestions, but against the general's orders. We were commanded to retreat into a barn, where we found thirty-nine regular army men, awaiting the breakout. We found the sharpshooters—who had overnighted there—pale, sleeping or lying around in the middle of the battle, while the blazing town of Grootschoote lit up the night sky and our men awaited relief. Finally the decision came from the artillery. Everyone was restless. Levi had thrown himself face-down across a nearby anthill, so as not to see or hear anything. Suddenly the signal: "Attack!" A yelled order from the colonel reaches us in the barn: "All sharpshooters to the attack!" Trumpets are sounded, men come out from behind ever fence and wall, the entire platoon advances rapidly and in orderly fashion to the burning town. A few regulars want to join the group. Bokelberg is in charge. Levi jumps up, bursting out angrily: "Are we sharpshooters?" The question works. It's clear to everyone that what he said is a sophism because the colonel has ordered: "All sharpshooters to the attack," informing us that we must join them as well. But the literal order only reads "sharpshooters," so none of us can blame ourselves if we interpret it to exclude the thirty-nine regulars. Everyone, down to the ambitious Bokelberg and two other comrades declare: "We stay where we lie;" this decision saves our lives, because every attempt fails.

Two days before his death, Levi was put up for the Iron Cross. Because high command had a bad conscience about the overhasty order which caused unnecessary deaths of many brave men, all survivors were considered for a decoration. All forms of merit were sought out, to give the survivors a "small consolation prize." But Levi was so extraordinarily sober-minded that he made it difficult for even the most well-meaning superiors to find an action which, as we used to say, "had the odor of bravery."

Events unfolded as follows: During Christmas, we were on guard duty in the trenches, when ration problems appeared. We were assigned meat rations but the impoverished towns lacked fodder and other animal food. It was a terrible thing to see how dogs, cats, poultry, sheep and cattle slowly starved to death, wandering around amongst the ruins, alternately tearing each other apart and pegging out by the wayside. There were plenty of pigs in our towns, but insufficient cattle, because entire herds had been driven ahead of us as protection against land mines. A sudden hideous cry, a terrible detonation, and we could march safely over the debris of a herd of several hundred cattle. By contrast, pigs roamed wild amongst the living and the dead.

A commission—on which Colonel von Krosigk served—was set up to examine how pigs could manage without corn, kitchen waste, and spent grain. Suddenly Levi stood up with his own brand of imperturbable anti-officer chutzpah. "See here Levi," said the colonel, "how are you doing?" The answer came: "How do you think? I'm still here don't you see?" "Yes, yes, I remember that night in October," said the old man, embarrassed in front of the two staff surgeons. "Nu, I remember it too," said Levi. "What does he want?" the colonel thought ungraciously. Levi burst out" "let 'em feed on corpses." The men looked at each other: wasn't Levi articulating what they themselves had already thought of but nor articulated out of a sense of revulsion? The colonel stared at Levi warily, chewing his moustache: "what d'you mean by that?" Levi replied tentatively, as if testing how far he could go: "enemy corpses, of course." The colonel spluttered scornfully, and the younger staff surgeon said: "Christian honor means a soldier's grave." Levi handed him a piece of paper with room for name and date, on which he had written: "The undersigned infantryman affirms that, if he is killed, the fatherland may use his body as pig swill." The senior surgeon thumped him on the shoulder: "You are a patriot, a true son of the fatherland!" "How can I be a patriot when I am dead?" asked Levi astonished. On the same day, he collected almost 300 signatures, testifying that, if the men died or were killed, they couldn't care less what was done with their bodies. However, these testamentary instructions were not accepted. Both chaplains were appalled and fought against them, treating Levi with contempt. The colonel was of the opinion that an observant Jew who agreed to use his body for pig swill loved his fatherland so much that he was worthy of the Iron Cross. But in the meanwhile, Levi died. The details of what happened are as follows:

That day, we came under unsuccessful machine gun and mortar fire. During the evening we were relieved for a few days and took up quarters in an electric company, set up cozily for Christmas. No: now it strikes me that it was a paper factory, not an electric company, in whose rooms we had established electricity and even connection by bells. We were in very good spirits. British trenches were not far, and we thought that we could see their high-lying entrenchment structure from our window. The night was clear and cold, with a starry sky. There was supposed to be an upcoming Christmas truce. We wrapped ourselves up in our coats. Many men had separate sleeping quarters; I shared mine with Levi.

Suddenly a single, far-away, gruesome scream penetrated my half-awake state. The room was moon bright, and I saw Levi siting in bed listening. What was going on? A dying horse was whinnying piteously somewhere in the vicinity of the British entrenchments.[11] Suddenly Levi's body was racked by a crying fit: I silently turned to the wall. We all recognize such hours: maybe he was thinking of a young girl, or small siblings at home. When something like this occurs, we help each other and try not to notice. We all feel the same fate: terrible and unavoidable. Levi roared: "Brutes! Blackguards! Scoundrels!" "Wow! What on earth has gotten into you?" I asked. "Animals! Beasts!" he roared. "Who? The British?" "No, everyone! You!" I replied, much offended. "What did I do during the war to offend you?" "You are also from the beautiful old city of Hanover," he said somewhat more calmly, stood up and started to dress leisurely. "What are you getting at?" I asked, but he ignored me, continuing: "To hell with your cursed hero's death. It's all a hoax." I thought that he was ill, and deep inside sensed that something was very wrong, but didn't move. He took his revolver, said "I whistle at a hero's death," and walked outside. I was so groggy from tiredness that I thought: "He's not talking sense; Leave him alone and he'll come right." I listened carefully for any night sounds: nothing stirred, and I slowly fell asleep. I started up at midnight: shots rang out behind the woods. One, then more, first from the British, then answered by our side.

I fell asleep again, tossing and turning from terrible dreams of what was going on outside almost every night. When I woke in the morning I thought about Levi again. He wasn't at roll call. No one knew where he was: some thought that he had shot himself. Two days later, what had happened became clear. We found him when our troops took the northern part of the English positions, shot through by several bullets next to a giant horse cadaver. When I reflected on what happened that night, I again heard the terrible cry of the horse in torment, which represented the suffering and misery of all mankind. The scream made Levi frantic, more than the others who could hear it and kept on sleeping. He must have succeeded in creeping out despite the snowy night, to put the horse out of its misery. But by doing so he alerted the enemy and, when he wanted to return, they shot him dead. How could such a logical, thinking man die such a senseless death?

Endnotes

1   Theodor Lessing, *Feind im Land. Satiren und Novellen* (Hannover: Wolf Albrecht Adam Verlag, 1923), 149–171.

2   Alexander von Kluck (1846–1934), German general, commander of the First Army, the strong right wing on the outer western edge of the German advance through Belgium and France; Paul von Hindenburg (1847–1934), German field marshal commanding the German Imperial Army during World War I; Otto von Emmich (1848–1915), major general commanding the Army of the Meuse which laid siege to and conquered the fortress of Liège on 16 August, 1914; Karl von Bülow (1846–1921), German field marshal commanding the German Second Army during between 1914 and 1915; Helmuth von Moltke the Younger (1848–1916), General and Chief of the German General Staff during 1914.

3   Stargard (Poland).

4   Kaliningrad (Russia).

5   Lessing served as physician during World War I. Although he finished his medical studies, he never sat for the examination.

6   Unless one is a diabetic, sugar lozenges are not harmful to the health, except for the teeth.

7   A reference to Siegfried in *Das Niebelungenlied* and Wagner's opera of that name.

8   A Belgian town in the province of Liège.

9   French for «free shooters," a term for irregular military, applied to formations deployed by France during the Franco-Prussian War (1870–1871). These guerrilla attacks had a profound effect on the German General Staff. During World War I: they carried out a harsh and severe occupation of areas which they conquered. Occupying German forces were fearful of spontaneous civil resistance, which led to arrests and preemptive executions. Most attacks attributed to Belgian *francs-tireurs* were carried out by Belgian Army snipers, or mistaken German fire.

10 Grootschotte.

11 Strictly speaking, a dying horse does not scream, but rather whinnies harrowingly.

5

Episode, 1916[1]

Russet evening shades descended on the violated forests of La Varennes, as the last beams of sunlight trickled away in the black clouds of gunpowder over the ashen fields. Artillery fire stopped for a few hours, and soldiers on both sides camped in the dugouts, smoking, drinking, dreaming or chattering. Coal-covered, mud-spattered animal-figures, stuffed dully together into dugouts for the past 3 months, now released for a few hours into a ghost-like, half-dream state. Seven hours' march away, well-fortified German positions surrounded the three occupied towns of Doutrepont, Aigles and Turenne, and extended into the vicinity of the small Turenne woods—where all birdsong had been stilled—and the wide Varennes plains. A giant net of communications trenches, tunnels and passageways, supported with planks, cement, and revetments and including comfortable shelters and sleeping quarters, crisscrossed the area.

In *one* specific section, one of our saps came within 80 meters of the French trenches, so that men could hear each other cursing and singing. On either side, fences had been fashioned out of barbed wire, and bodies lay in the open field between wide, gaping craters. Corpses were thrown over the wire, so as not to take up space in the trenches and poison the air. However, an unwritten agreement had been made on both sides for a few gallant souls to crawl out at night during breaks in the fighting, and bury their fallen comrades lying in what we called the "field of corpses"—French beside German, enemy beside enemy. Guns chattered up again valiantly across the mounds of earth, and the wooden fir cross decorated with rowanberries, planted by a faithful German for some or other dead comrade, gleamed blood red in the lurid light of the searchlight. Sepp Stiglmeir, *Landsturm* man[2] from Ingolstadt, who blew the bugle so splendidly at evening taps, was stationed in this section. His clear notes were the signal for replacement troops, who had marched 45 minutes from the first line of trenches just for the privilege of sleeping for a few hours in protected dugouts. How everyone longed for that! But this evening, although replacements were ready, there was no signal from Stiglmeir.

In the meanwhile, men hung around in their dugouts. From airplanes, they looked like giant wagon ruts, or furrows in which a black species of flea beetles hopped around tirelessly. The east wind slowly cooled the lovely evening peace, wafting in dreamy images which quietly hovered over, covering and dazzling us with a wave of homesickness. A caravan of comforting souls appeared: a cherry blossom tree branch tapping on the window of a father's house, the Jacob's well at the linden tree outside the town, dreamy houses on the Rhine, the faraway face of a North German grandmother, a sweet blond child's face with blue eyes—German eyes.[3]

A few groups gathered for the inevitable round of three-man skat. Some exchanged cigarettes, smoking material, and snuff tobacco. Many resoled their boots, and coarse hands without number tinkered with, riveted, and hammered embrasure planks, or assembled and cleaned bayonet and rifle. Everyone knew that they were about to launch a great offensive, to once and for all clean out the French trenches across the "field of dead."[4]

During these last hours we could also write letters or make our wills, grumble or dream, drink or pray. Each recognized his own individual duty.

The Valkyries, female harvesters of death, flew over the faithful men, kissing them secretly, like trees marked by the forester to be cut

down tomorrow.[5] But, even the evening before the battle, the boister-
ous mood didn't change. Dusk always brought dizzy carefreeness—men
laughed for no discernable reason. Was it because another mindless day
had just passed, bringing them one day closer to the end one way or the
other? Was it that they were still alive after death had reaped such a rich
harvest earlier today?

The replacement men assembled in tightly packed formations. They
fooled around, chaffed each other, spat, chewed tobacco, and waited for
the signal. As always, the dull soldiers' words buzzed in the air, a manner of speaking drummed into them over weeks and months. Couplets,
tacky operetta songs sung wisely to themselves and laughed over point-
lessly times without number, From somewhere, the "German Stiglmeir
March" began, and soon the whole trench was humming:

> Oh our life here in the muddy trench
> Is not a pleasant life by any means
> For breakfast we have lead instead of beans[6]
> And at noontime there'll be more for lunch.
> Then when evening comes and twilight falls
> Stiglmeir goes in front of all
> He can do tarantaratara
> As no other in this army can.
> As no other in this army can.

Suddenly the brisk tempo faltered! Men approached the embrasures. Something unusual seemed to be happening above, in the "field of
the dead," in front of the entrance to French trenches. A bullet sparked
here and there. The fiery balls rattled, greeting each other in the air like
flaming serpents, finding their mark somewhere in or near our trenches.

What could we see? A lone man stood in the "field of the dead," this
side of the barbed wire about 50 meters away, surrounded by whizzing
bullets, rising powerfully against the grey-red evening sky. He staggered
forward slowly across the multitude of mole-like craters. Some thought
they saw his helmeted head emerging carefully. Others reported that his

hands clawed at the dark trench and that, crawling on his belly through the barbed wire, he miraculously managed to escape the gruesome field of corpses. A defector, a snitch—probably a madman.

As the figure approached, we recognized a delicate, unhelmeted, weaponless little man. He had wild, black, wavy hair and staring, crazy eyes and was making incomprehensible signs. Obviously a madman who must have somehow escaped from the battlefield.

A hand grenade whooshed, and the madman's flapping arm fell back slackly. We watched the scene breathlessly. A few shots appeared from the far end of the trench, and the pale little man slumped down like a folded up pocket knife, lying like a colored stain on the pale ground. We imagined that we heard mad whimpering, and saw his red blood seep into the grey rocks.

"He's had it!" the German soldiers said. This was the usual satisfied expression that German soldiers used, to declare that yet another enemy had been shot down.

But look! Like a wild demon, the fallen man hauled himself up with deliberate strength, staggered, fell again, and crawled over the newly ploughed field. He yelled, gesticulated and beckoned while bullets flew around him, desperately waving his bleeding arm stump.

On the same field of corpses where the unfortunate man[7] was flapping around like a sail in the wind, two German soldiers noticed someone else through their binoculars. Yes! He was clearly visible! A second man was crawling forward on his belly towards the German trenches, in constant danger of being hit by one side or the other in the open field. Was he a Frenchman or a German? Those with sharp eyes saw by his uniform that he was German and, as he gradually got closer, his grey Bavarian tunic became obvious. Suddenly someone cried out definitely: "It's Stiglmeir!"

Little Lieutenant von Lieven, pale and excited, danced frantically along the trench, tore the soldiers away from the embrasures, and yelled: "Don't shoot! Don't shoot! Don't shoot!" Our attention turned to a distant section of trench behind the edge of the woods. Here and there a shot roared from the German section, which was not returned by the

French. A few men did gymnastics on the trench rim, but the more circumspect yelled: "Be careful! Get down! They want to lure us out, and bump us off in the open field!"

A dead quiet gradually enveloped us. Troops gathered round lookout holes, staring intently at the crawling German and enigmatic Frenchman. The Frenchman picked himself up, fell, picked himself up again and again until he reached the site where Stiglmeir lay. The German, apparently seriously wounded, struggled hopelessly, twisting and turning like a cut up earth worm.

All sorts of suspicious forms now emerged from the French trenches. Kepis, beards, faces, entire bodies. One Frenchman sat astride the grey earthen wall, waving to the Germans. Very suspicious: was this not the enemy who, in a few short hours, must be impaled on German bayonets? Was this a ruse? A trap? After three victorious months, should one believe that French front line troops would stop fighting, just to save Sepp Stiglmeir from Ingolstadt?

German non-commissioned officers held their troops back. Nothing must be undertaken without clear orders from higher up.

Quiet, thoughtful Captain Krûger, *also* a Bavarian, came out of his dugout to see what was happening. He carried the *Tapferkeitsmedaille*[8] on his chest, and the Iron Cross in the buttonhole of his hastily donned Litewka[9] jingled against the empty uniform buttons. "What's going on?" he asked calmly. "The Frenchman is bringing Stilgmeir in!" stammered the soldier at the nearest embrasure, half paralyzed with fright.

The captain pushed the soldier roughly aside, looked over the field for a few moments, and ordered him to bend down. He stood on the man's back, leaped out of the trench with the aid of two other men, and stood free in the open field, exposed to French rifle fire. The French guns were silent, and the captain walked forward unhesitatingly.

When the men saw what their captain had done they themselves couldn't be held back, and soon the entire company had climbed out and stood in the open field. In the meanwhile, the bleeding, badly injured Frenchman laboriously dragged the half-dead Stiglmeir behind him, like a heavy, harpooned whale. Soon German medical orderlies carefully took charge of the badly wounded man. The staff surgeon firmly cut open the man's uniform and dressed Stiglmeir's wound with cloth. French soldiers swarmed around, and soldiers from both sides looked at each other with amazement. The German captain stood firm and calmly in front of the daring Frenchman who, pale and bleeding, could hardly stand upright. But, with good army discipline, he placed his mutilated arm on his trouser seams, and reported: "François Dilloyer from Rouen, *ouvrier* [workman]." Not knowing how to control his surging emotions or what to say, Krüger tore the Iron Cross with its ribbon from his Litewka button, and began with clumsy, trembling hands to attach it to the Frenchman's uniform. Modest pride shone in the Frenchman's eyes. German orderlies helped him out of his kit, and bandaged his shot up arm.

"A workman from Rouen!" flew from mouth to mouth. No further explanation was required, because everyone sensed what had happened. This young Frenchman had seen from his trench that one man was marooned amongst a sea of corpses, fired on from both sides in a vain attempt to somehow struggle back to his Bavarian troops from the grisly battlefield. Dilloyer had tried to make the Germans aware of their man, but, when he saw that this was hopeless, he used an evening cessation in hostilities to risk his own life, in an effort to return the wounded German to his company.

They all understood this. Although his heroic performance appeared as unbelievable as it was pointless, everyone wanted to see this enemy soldier and show him a friendly gesture. It was the first time that the hardened men from both sides, packed together cheek by jowl in the trenches for three months, had thought of anything but outsmarting, wounding, and firing rounds off at the enemy. For the first time they really looked closely at one other, and were almost surprised to see that, under the crust of mud and dirt, they all had the same white human faces, dirtied by gunpowder and earth, defiled by the dogs of war and human hate. After a few dumb, astonished moments, they suddenly burst out into wild, ungovernable laughter. They laughed so much that tears rolled down their faces. It was as if they gained sudden insight into a vast world comedy, and could only free themselves from the uneasy burden of a human pack animal by a fit of glorious laughing, which suddenly removed all care. Because they couldn't understand each other's language, they shook hands trustingly and told each other their names and civilian occupations. And so, in one part of a field of corpses, two tailors met, in another two locksmiths three cobblers, or a few farmer's sons. With nervous excitement, they began to exchange experiences and dreams. "How many cattle?" one man asked in German. The other raised ten fingers, indicating in French that he had ten cows in his father's barn. Without further ado, they named their children and beloveds, understanding everything without the help of language. They called each other "*Du*"[10] and "*Kamerad*"[11] as if they were old comrades, on the same vulnerable ship of misery. They noticed that they had the same customs and exchanged cigarettes, snuff and smoking tobacco, laughing because one of them was too fat, the other too lean...

In the meanwhile, the sun set on the shot up gloomy ashen fields. The drawn out, mournful sound of taps, echoing warningly over the woods of La Turenne, urged the Germans to return to their foxholes. After only a few hours of sleep, the great offensive was to thunder over the field of corpses on which they had previously stood in cozy chitchat with the coming night's mortal enemies. The sound brought them back to the realities of war, that it was high treason to utter a word about what was forbidden to say even amongst themselves, but what they all knew would happen this night.

Lieutenant von Lieven, short both in stature and original ideas, bubbled over with meaningless French words, bounding from one mortal enemy to the other with tears running down his cheeks. For him, this was the high point of his young life.

Captain Krüger stood silently like a stone hero. No! Like a poor sinner, caught in the act. His plain brown hair suddenly seemed to have turned grey and his face was as ashen as the hideously shot up field of corpses in the late evening twilight. Suddenly he pulled himself together, commanding sternly and inexorably in a toneless voice: "To your guns!"

The men stood undecided for a moment. Was mutiny in the air? They looked around wildly and stubbornly. German soldiers gave French soldiers their hand, and said ingenuously: "Well, go with God comrade. All the best, and Auf Wiedersehen." But they suddenly reflected on what they had said and, like improbable masks in a comedy, grinned and exploded with laughter again. For a fleeting moment, lifted above space and time, these doomed, abused men, sensing the darkness that was to come, laid their heavy, tired, calloused worker's hands on one another's shoulders. They looked into each other's empty eyes with great seriousness and, on the ash-grey barren field of corpses on which the first stars shone, some men even kissed one another.

In the meanwhile, Stiglmeir's wounds were dressed and he was loaded onto a stretcher prior to transportation to a rear echelon hospital. His savior, the young Dilloyer, was bandaged: his mutilated arm would have to be properly amputated by French doctors. He came, half-carried, half-supported by his comrades, to take leave of the captain and thank him for the Iron Cross. The captain shook his head silently. Everyone climbed back into their respective trenches, to do their duty for their countries. The artillery began to open up: in the farthermost positions, those in charge had become wary, and the nearest German major sent runners with strictest instructions for the men to get back to their positions at once. All conversation with French soldiers was to cease forthwith, on pain of death.

This section of trench must be sacrificed, and the brave troops must die for the fatherland tonight. But on which side would the men die?

But first they lay down to rest—Germans and Frenchmen alike. East and west winds slowly cooled the lovely, mild evening peace, wafting in dreamy images which quietly covered us, hovering over and dazzling us with a wave of homesickness. A caravan of comforting souls appeared before us: a cherry blossom tree branch tapping on the window of a father's house, the Jacob's well at the linden tree outside the town, dreamy houses on the Rhine and Loire, faraway faces of South German and Provençal grandmothers or, in the far distance, a pair of sweet blond and black haired childrens' faces with blue eyes—dark

eyes—German eyes—French eyes—The night was heavy with dread—
wireless telegrams sped through the trenches: thoughts and commands
from the all-powerful general staff. The Kaiser's last greeting to the
doomed. Orderlies arrived with skittering lanterns. Shadows flittered,
and black wings flapped over the plain. Somewhere in the distance the
eerie sound of laughter sounded. A hoot owl screeched at midnight in
the little wood of La Turenne, where the sound of birds hadn't been
heard for months. A pale, milky mist floated over the field of corpses,
and a silvery death barque sailed over the milky sea. A layer of blue gla-
cial ice shivered on the enigmatic, corpse-like moon.

Very few Germans returned from that night attack. Captain Krüger,
who led the charge, was the first to fall. The foolish little Lieutenant von
Lieven also died bravely. The few who returned after cleaning the French
out of that section of trench spread an unbelievable rumor. They said
that, shortly before the command came "Fix bayonets! Over the top!"
everyone saw the figure of a man in the moonlight emerging from the
forest of La Turenne, dragging his foot like Dilloyer. He walked over the
battlefield, stopped for a long while at the wooden fir cross decorated
with blood-red rowanberries, and then disappeared into the mist. On
his head he wore a crown of thorns.

Endnotes

1   Theodor Lessing, *Feind im Land. Satiren und Novellen* (Hannover: Wolf Albrecht Adam Verlag, 1923), 173–186.

2   Militia or military units composed of troops of inferior quality.

3   German myth places great importance on trees and rivers, especially the Rhine.

4   No man's land.

5   The Valkyries were each of Odin's twelve handmaidens who conducted the slain warriors of their choice from the battlefield to Valhalla.

6   *Blaue Bohnen.*

7   Lessing refers to him as a Frenchman for the first time two paragraphs later.

8   World War I medal for bravery awarded by several individual German states, including Bavaria.

9   Double-breasted, coat-like uniform jacket.

10   German colloquial "you."

11   Comrade.

6

Prisoner's Greeting, 1923[1]

My brothers, you light-streaming brothers,
Clouds, banks, water, winds so fair
Eyes of the earth, creatures small,
Light-winged moths of dew and air,
Locked behind stonewalled shackles' pain
My life was waning, chain-sick, flat.
You brought back dreams and beauty to me
Thanks for that, thanks for that.

Comrades! You have sent me a small, blue flower.[2] The first flower that has grown on the fortress farm in Niederschönenfeld, Rain am Lech, Bavaria since the war.

For a short light-filled hour, released from the grave's iron grip – you Gustav Klingelhöfer or you Ernst Toller[3]—your young eyes have spotted a modest blue winter flower under building rubble, covered with snow.

One of you has said: "We'll send it to Theodor Lessing." During the long years in jail, you have joined my readership. The first and perhaps my only ones, but no thinker had two better readers at the time.

You have correctly sensed: this man belongs to us, we caged-in German youth!

I received your letter in Hanover on a sullen winter morning, I found the little harbinger of spring pressed into it, and regarded it with an almost religious awe.

Yes, we are all spawned from the earth too early: young and cocky, under building rubble, covered with snow.

We will die before roses bloom in Germany again, and not experience the hot July nights that bless the seeds of our homeland.

Revolutionaries? Yes, but real conservatives as well. Because we preserve our near-original state of nature in the midst of sophisticated, well-adjusted civilized humanity, like blue flowers breaking through the rubbish heap of a prison yard.

I placed the wrinkled flower in hot water, in which it opened. While I sat at my desk in the back room of the noisy city house, my gaze wandered over its walls and chimneys. A delicate, gentle fragrance wafted over me into the bare day.

What do you, simple flower, have to tell the prisoners?

I would like to be your human mouthpiece. Because I am afforded no other expression but abstract philosophical concepts, I must try to begin the thought process of *that* life in which you, blue Easter flower, breathe but remain so silent.

A poet says "flowers are the earth's dreams."[4] This is true in its purest sense.

The world of transfiguration (the Indian *brâhma vidya*) is the dream of chthonic elements.[5]

All "realities in space and time" have their origin in *dreams*, and vice versa: Dream images must constantly knock on the iron gates of reality.

Shadows press onto the earth's heart. They want to drink blood, in order to speak with human voices.

Their germ lies in the clods of the prison cell. Must not everything that sprouts from it, visibly and as a fully-formed shape, first be dreamed up metaphorically and in image form?[6]

The dry, stiff, yellowish acorn contains in it the seeds of an oak tree. The corn field that nourishes all mankind dreams inside the insignificant wheat kernel. The bird's liberating motion and liberated song lies sleeping in the colorless ice dungeon. The insignificant caterpillar, crawling as if imprisoned from leaf to leaf (like the soul from generation to generation, from form to form) pupates and becomes invisible, only to fly away at the first joyful sunny hour, in the new form of an ether-light, beautiful, multicolored butterfly.

Plato's wisdom coins a word for this clear but secret concept: idea. In German, this means vision or image.[7]

Plato teaches that visions or images cannot be sought in space or time. They can therefore also not be found in conscious reality, or in the temporal and spatial moving world. Entities (ideas) are not *real* in a spatial (physical) or temporal (historical) sense.

Nevertheless, we humans have the capability of *perceiving* this unreal sphere. We call this perception "reason." Thanks to it, we can fly into the realm of the spaceless and timeless.

A certain yearning in our heart holds us back from flight into the realm of utopia. Plato calls this eros.[8]

This eros forces us to *transform* what we see in the mind into earthly things.

The yearning for realization inspires us.

Everything we call reality (the entire spatial and temporal conscious world) is: realization, processing,[9] objectification, reification, determination, and definition of the "idea world" into a second *artificial* world, in other words the actuality of our human actions, values, and words.

Our world of humanity, together with sun, moon, and stars, is thus nothing but a mechanical *synthesis* of life and ideas, thus a polar *reflection* of transcendent consciousness. In this consciousness, *on the other side of* space, time and movement, idea and life are organically *one*.

This is how Plato explained the creative secret.

With this metaphor, he compared the "world" to dancing shadows, which fall onto the walls of our prison cells from light beings whose life grows and exists outside and beyond our cell.

The shadows whose dreams we are, are images of our spiritual home. Our homesickness. Our wanderlust. Our eternal present. This is the secret:

That human consciousness has broken out of life's element, thanks to distress and necessity.

This being in the "existence"[10] of a *world* is reflected inside consciousness (as movement, movement repositories and spatio-temporality) in the forms that shape consciousness.

What, therefore, is "world?"

Realization of ideas in the life element.

Life—reality—truth: these are three eternally separated spheres. Bur *our* sphere is—reality!

Every human generation has guessed at this riddle: a riddle that in reality is no riddle at all.

In Plato's school, the realm of images pertained as an omnipresent, inactive world of existence[11] *behind* reality.

But already in Aristotle's more empirically based school, the world of essences was pulled down and into the sphere of historical-temporal reality.[12]

Now ideas became valid as *natural* creative impulses.

A few centuries later (under the cross of naturally spiritual and humanized Christianity), images became spirit.

Augustine called them canons or norms. Life's images were now ideals of reason, in other the words the *human self*.[13]

Differences of opinion ran wild.

For one, they were timeless larvae of being.[14] For the other they were abstract concepts.

For Plotinus, they were gods without number, looking at him.[15] For Augustine, they were postulates of God's one and only holy spirit. All called it the realm of ideas!

This idea realm came, for some, *before* all experience. For others, it came *out of*, and *thanks to*, experience, and for yet others, it was only *real in* those who experienced it.

The idea was sometimes one, sometimes the other, often both together.

This touches on the nub of an enormous *human deception*.

The deception has ended in our time.

The so-called cultured and civilized people of Europe and the Americas have reinforced the great self-deception. Their own, logical-ethical world of human ideas is *consubstantial* with the eternal presence of form.

Wherever we hear the words idea, form, structure, entity, image today, they refer to some form of *conceptual* observation and view.[16] Since the time of Descartes, this half-megalomaniacal self- deception of the metamorphosis of humans to cosmos, making each individual a cosmos unto himself, has held sway.[17]

The nucleus of this deception is the illusion that life is *thinking*![18] Antecedents or contents of consciousness are *living*! Therefore, everything living must be temporally conceivable as "movement" or "occurrence." Thus, a man can ascend to objective degrees of value and rank, and become a "superior" natural being. However, while ascending degrees of rank like platforms of a pyramid, it becomes possible for "objective developmental levels" not to reflect the "bearer's" existence and life.

I append below several examples of the dreamless, unworldly abuse by "civilization" of eidos[19] and ideas.

We find this abuse in Germany especially where the spirit of Hegel, that great gravedigger of our national myth, still lives.[20] Hegel exchanged human orientation of living with living itself: the motionless being[21] with temporal *historical* event sequences. He used the old word "idea" to define that deadest and most meaningless of abstractions, his "Absolute Spirit."

A true disciple of my teacher Schopenhauer, I have labored my entire life to shoo away this spectral dance.[22]

This self-righteous illusion of so-called educated humanity is the current fashion. Life is defined as a linear temporal continuum, like an ascending pyramid or sliding spiral. *Being*[23] is not differentiated anymore, but rather *degree*!

Those who reawaken Hegel and Oswald Spengler (like all national and state theoreticians) treat cultures and civilizations as if they were *organisms*—confusing the world of form with the history of progress—without conscientiously asking where the body of civilization manifestly blossoms and dies.[24]

Yes, certainly! It is easy to call the blue flower—as well as the whole of Germany—an organism. But even the most uncritical intellect must clearly see that nations, states and civilizations are not the same *life forms* as plants or animals.

Despotic academic philosophy in our German universities does even more mischief, mixing mythical symbols with terminology.

They speak of phenomena and phenomenology. What do they *mean* by that?

Not the living flower, but rather. its perception, thought and experience are the true phenomena!

They prattle about observation, view, intuition, immediacy. What do they *mean* by that?

Hairsplitting dialectical conceptual dissection! Definition, arithmetization, determination, by which the living growth of all languages on earth is devitalized, and the psychic is allowed to congeal into psychology

Gravestones and urns of former lives, no! Inscriptions on these stones and urns will be presented under false flags, as eidetic vision and life synopsis.

I can explain this great deception more comprehensibly and clearly, by referring to the modern science of life, so called biology,

This science clearly reveals that what we think as living beings must represent a type of movement in time, in other words mechanics. Nowhere is this more honestly and clearly shown than for example by August Weismann, who fearlessly thinks that life is composed of atoms and sub-atoms which he calls "ides."[25]

Even the closest to life and most imaginative of our thinkers, Friedrich Nietzsche, didn't find a way out of the prison called modern science.[26]

He converted Dionysus into dynamics.[27]

How did he characterize life?

Life for him was something moved and moving. An enormous energy, will to power, taking possession of oneself, and self-overcoming. The Übermensch overcomes himself, not others.

He even derives "values" from growth quanta and tries to capture qualities through numbers.

That is the way to death!

Life is never movement, never temporal. Never decomposable or composable. Never comprehensible in thought. But it dreams in the eternal present of this blue flower...

Horrible! Utterly horrible, how the strong-willed have allowed themselves for millennia to be harried into the dead-end concept of "the spirit" and confused the calm, chaste life with one energized by will or passion, how they have come to *equate* formal and forming processes with creative structure.

Otto Weininger, a spiritual believer in this mold, carried Kantian-Fichtean sophistry, and every German idealistic thought, to mad extremes. He had the insane phantasy of turning the changing world of form into an incarnated ethical-logical dialectic. Life to morals.[28]

A no less important artistic figure, Jakob Wassermann, included artefacts with living forms like "you" and flowers together. He threw everything into one pot: forms, structures, ideas, ideals, norms, fictions, concepts.[29]

One sees this secret confusion of the worthless with life in the fact that all these poor sinners *preach*, and studiously disregard, everything that creates human *grandeur*: intellect, science, critique.

I always remember the anecdote from the life of Charles Darwin. The great naturalist was considered England's greatest son, alongside Thomas Carlyle. Their respective disciples worked together, to bring England's greatest naturalist and greatest philosopher together. Darwin decided to visit Carlyle. "How did it go?" he was asked. "An intolerable human being," Darwin said. "I sat there for three hours while he spoke uninterruptedly at me about "the power of holy silence."[30]

The honest immediacy of life lives in *one* area: that of strictest unreality, in other words pure theory.

Theories…the word alone means vision or Weltschau [intuition of the world]. One sign of this, is that human language is completely dependent on the eye. The primeval gift of the seer, that visionary unbound by the real world who could epitomize the "unimaginable, eternal," was for the ancients: theory.

The word "theory" is related to *theoi*, the Greek word for gods, but also with theater—the Weltschau in which the gods behind the world become visible in ecstasy. *This* Weltschau is theory as well. Think about that, you young poets!

The capability and eidetic vision of the gods—theoretical reason— is mankind's eternal, or as they say "godly," share.

But the capability of ideas and ideals only allows us enter the "realm of eternal womanhood" with the help of Mephisto, the demon who has made understanding and will his own.

He can (as the parable of Faust says) give us the key to the "realm of eternal womanhood," but only our spiritual being can descend into it.[31]

God builds on this with his devil's wager. He confidently leaves this world, together with the human soul, to the devil's games, without the need to interfere. God trusts humanity, because man carries in himself a utopian spark of Godliness. But the devil (to whom the world belongs) neither senses nor pays attention to this. At the end of the day, he doesn't feel that this unreality remains the most real.

"These are but utopian dreams" says the devil. Even today, these are his favorite earthly words.

It is intrinsically true that we are all nothing but the incarnation of dreams. Children of the god "fancy," phantasy.

The world dreams itself. It is effectuating the power of dreams.

Like a small, alert island, surrounded by an immeasurable sea of dreams, waking consciousness and its temporospatial reality have risen up for a short interval of time from the dark utopian torrent.

When sleep comes, my ego[32] sinks from me, and dumb images arise, it seems as if everything that we want and think during daylight hours is a lie. Our thoughts revolve around things that will not exist in

10.000 years. Only the realm of night is real. If we call everything that lives "God," then you, o small flower, are nearer to God than my spirit with all its logic and ethics, life's wrong, dead-end way.

This is the blue pennywort's first pronouncement. "I am the effect of a dream, the body of utopia. Life sends me upwards, and the men who have been imprisoned for years in the Bavarian Niederschönenfeld fortress send it on to you, to release the soul of utopia from their cage."

O tremendous power of dreams! Throw down a fragment, a shell of yourself, and tomorrow it will be overgrown with age, moss, fungi, microbes. Nothing in the world is dead. Where there is opportunity, the power of dreams drives *form* forth. There are no gradual levels. All levels flower, all follow with and beside each other. Man's powers to create, regulate, build are nothing but the weak reflection of this romancing dream passion.

But why, o flower, don't you remain in timeless, spaceless darkness? Why this thirst for fruition in the light? Why this sham, this emergence and beauty?

An age-old Doric choral song begins "Beauty wants love."

We know this from Plato's legacy. He solves the purpose of realization by proof that the purpose of all beauty is to unfetter the creative power of love. Behind the transformative world of appearances burns the procreative, redemptive spirit of *eros*.

Do you not feel the Easter myth of the Risen Christ?

The small flower from the prison solves the Easter riddle. Its silence grows out of the depths of Germanic prehistory.

Gerda, the earth maiden—the Brunnhild of the heroic legend,[33] the Briar Rose of the children's story—is imprisoned by the terrible powers of darkness. The sapient ice giants, the Jöturn, hold her gagged, but she secretly lives son, dreaming of redemption.[34]

The dreams of yearning burning within her can he realized and redeemed in blooming gardens and great forests, in flowers, meadows, and blessed corn. They cannot bloom or be fulfilled so long as the all-wise Jöturns rule the earth and the Messiah is far away.

Only one way remains for Gerda: she must give him a sign.

So she collects all her feminine life-giving power and changes them into spiritual force. She lets this spiritual aura *shine*, as a beacon over all nations and lands.

The Northern Lights!

This myth emits primeval awe. It contains the primeval soul: the innumerable colors of the Northern Lights, blue, red-gold, silver-white, violet, brown (physics construes these as resulting from earth magnetism). The primeval world saw in them the power of love. The yearning outstretched arms of the gagged, captured earth goddess radiate these wonders into all flower gardens that sleep undisturbed in her bosom, so that Baldur the god of spring—the mythical Siegfried—can return from happier sunny climes and free her, shattering Jöturn's icy chains with his sword, the sunbeam.[35]

The Northern Lights shine over the earth, giving him a sign.

"I love you," they call out. "I yearn for you. Come, redeemer, kiss your children. Look here. They *could,* and will, bloom, but only when *you* awaken them to light in my bosom."

Baldur sees beauty's torch. He waves and entices from the land of the bright and blond. They are the color of his sons.

As the colors of the Northern Lights are the reflection of the earth's flowers, so is what we see as ideas the reflection of being.

We think of an ideal as that which the earth yearns to fulfil. What tempts us as an idea is the *spiritual anticipation* of the kingdom that wishes to, and will come, but only insofar as *we* come to it and love its beauty.

The realm of ideas covers both Klingelhöfer's theories, and Toller's theater. It is the *same* light that shines in structural form, when love redeems it. You, small flower, blossom and keep silent just as humans do.

That is the second announcement of the Niederschönenfeld prison flower.

Soon it will soon be Easter. Humanity's belief in miracles dimly intuits infinite simplicity: the correlation between spirit and life. The relationship between beauty and love. Ancient myth saw the dreams of flowers slumbering in the earth in the colors of the Northern Lights. These flowery dreams glow in heaven as symbols of yearning for a redemptive God. Only a trace of *this* symbol has remained for us.

We hide Easter eggs for our children in gardens that are still bare. Multicolored, iridescent eggs. Small children look for them during days blessed with the newly beginning springtime of life.

Like the ice-encrusted earth, the egg is both a grave and a cell. In the egg, just as in the prison cell, the living yearns for redemption. On the feast of Resurrection, faith inspired, we paint lovely, joyful colors and lights on the egg's hard shell. Our faith in Easter leads us to believe that, miraculously, the grave opens up and the heavy stone is rolled aside. Christ is redeemed and, redeeming, flies up to heaven.

Have I answered and humanized your loveliness, small blue flower from the fortress yard?

Your leaves droop painfully. Your little head, scarcely raised, is already withered and tired. You will die during the course of this spring day.

You have a third thing to entrust to me before you die.

I have spoken of the beauty of Easter flowers and fragrance released into the air. I have spoken of the nature of love and life's compulsion towards love. Now you warn me: don't forget the gospel of pain.

Don't forget that this entire dream world, in space, time and all its beauty, is nothing but *an emergency exit for a trapped life.*

Don't forget that, with demolition of the prison and Jöturn's demise, the power of beauty-creating *yearning* also falls away: life-willing dreaming *transforms* into will and spirit.

Strange! A third metaphor rises out of the dying flower. It is an extension of the parable of nature's flames, the dance of the Northern Lights, the artificial but conscious color interplay of human hope and yearning, when we paint eggs for our children.

This third metaphor seems to lie in between the other two. The display of color in the change of seasons. The color play when the earth goddess sinks down again in the fall, and the forest blazes up one last time. It unites the palette of the entire year whereby bird feathers, calyces attracting butterflies and buds that need reproduction, even the skin and fur of animals, shine forth with all the colors of conflict, hate, love, and death.

A peculiar game was played at the gluttonous tables of Roman capitalists during the celebratory orgies of a dying society of plunderers and exploiters, at the start of the Christian era.

The magic of beauty, whose disappearing life courts love and compassion one last time, became a source of enjoyment for a so-called cultured society, which became clueless and impious.

There exists in nature a small, lancet-formed fish named the goatfish. By pricking and goading, fingering and tormenting, it is goaded into wasting its life away in a dance of colors.

The tormented little creature dazzles with every-changing colors until it cannot anymore and, declining into ever more abstract grey, it exhausts itself to death.

I have read your books and letters, thoughts and work, my comrades in the Niderschönenfeld prison.

I understand the essence of the spirit.

Allow me to kiss you, little flower, as if my reverence kisses *in* you all the humility, naïveté, silence, and innocence in the world, which we have killed with spirit and actions.

You don't have to tell me anything more.

I have lived it.

In you all.

In you.[36]

Endnotes

1   Theodor Lessing, *Feind im Land. Satiren und Novellen* (Hannover: Wolf Albrecht Adam Verlag, 1923), 187–205.

2   The blue flower (*blaue Blume*) was a central symbol of inspiration for the Romanticism movement, and remains a motif in Western art today. It stands for desire, love, and metaphysical striving for the infinite and unreachable. It symbolizes hope and the beauty of things. German author Novalis (Georg Philipp Friedrich Freiherr von Hardenberg, 1772–1801) introduced the symbol into the Romantic movement through his unfinished story, "Heinrich von Ofterdingen": After contemplating a meeting with a stranger, the young Heinrich dreams of a blue flower which calls to him and absorbs his attention. This blue flower is meant to symbolize the deep and sacred longings of a poet's soul. Romantic poetry deals with longing; not a definite, formulated desire for some obtainable object, but a dim, mysterious aspiration, a trembling unrest, a vague sense of kinship with the infinite, and dissatisfaction with every form of earthly happiness. Thomas Carlyle (see note 27) asserted that the blue flower "is Poetry, the real object, passion and vocation of young Heinrich, which, through many adventures, exertions and sufferings, he is to seek and find." The theme of the blue flower was also used by German poets such as Joseph Freiherr von Eichendorff (1788–1857) and Adelbert von Chamisso (1781–1838) and painters such as Otto Runge (1777–1810)

3   Gustav Klingelhöfer (1888–1961), German politician of the SPD (German Social Democratic Party). He served in the German Army during World War I, and was elected member of his unit's soldier's council at the end of the war. Shortly after, he became chairman of the Worker's Council General Assembly. In 1918 he became Supreme Commander of the "German Red Army" under Ernst Toller. For the latter, he was sentenced in June 1919 to 5½ years imprisonment in the fortress of Niederschönenfeld; Ernst Toller (1893–1939), German left-wing playwright. He served for six days in 1919 as president of the short-lived Bavarian Soviet Republic, after which he became the head of its army. He was imprisoned for five years the fortress of Niederschönenfeld, for his part in the armed resistance in the Soviet Republic to the central government in Berlin

4   Ralph Waldo Emerson (1803–1882), *Hamatreya*: "The earth laughs in flowers."

5   Brahmavidya (derived from the Sanskrit words brahma and vidyā) is that branch of scriptural knowledge derived primarily through a study of the divine. Brahmvidya is the knowledge and spiritual knowledge of divine faith/God/

existence. Put together, it means knowledge of the mantra/absolute; chthonic: concerning, belonging to, or inhabiting the cosmic/ethereal world.

6 *Bildhaft, Bild.*

7 The Theory of Forms or Theory of Ideas is a philosophical theory, concept, or world-view, attributed to the Athenian philosopher Plato (428/427 or 424/423– 348/347 BCE), that the physical world is not as real or true as timeless, absolute, unchangeable ideas.

8 Utopia: Term coined by Sir Thomas More (1478–1535) for an imagined community or society that possesses highly desirable or nearly perfect qualities for its citizens; Eros: The Greek god of love and sex.

9 *Verwirklichen, Verwerklichen.*

10 *Sein, Bestehen.*

11 *Seinswelt.*

12 Aristotle (384–322 BCE), Greek philosopher and polymath during the Classical period in Ancient Greece.

13 Augustine of Hippo (354–430 CE) also known as Saint Augustine, theologian, philosopher, and the bishop of Hippo in Numidia, Roman North Africa; Human self: *menschlicher Selbst.*

14 *Sein.*

15 Plotinus ((204/5–270 CE), generally regarded as the founder of Neoplatonism and one of the most influential philosophers in antiquity after Plato and Aristotle.

16 *Schauen, anschauen.*

17 René Descartes (1596–1650), creative mathematician, important scientific thinker, and original metaphysician.

18 *Cogito ergo sum* (I think therefore I am) (Descartes).

19 A Greek term meaning "form", "essence", "type" or "species."

20 Georg Wilhelm Friedrich Hegel (1770–1831), German philosopher and leading figure of German idealism.

21 *Seiend.*

22 Arthur Schopenhauer (1788–1860), German philosopher and founder of an atheistic metaphysical and ethical system that rejected the contemporaneous ideas of German idealism.

23 *Das Sein.*

24 Oswald Spengler (1880–1936), German historian and philosopher of history.

25 August Weismann (1834–1914), German biologist and one of the founders of the science of genetics.

26 Friedrich Nietzsche (1844–1900), German philosopher, cultural critic, composer, poet, and philologist whose work exerted a profound influence on modern intellectual history.

27 Dionysus: Greek god of wine and festivity.

28 Otto Weininger (1880–1903) Austrian thinker who lived in the Austro-Hungarian Empire. In 1903, he published the book *Geschlecht und Charakter* (Sex and Character), which gained popularity after his suicide. See Theodor Lessing, *Der Jüdischer Selbsthass* (Berlin; Jüdischer Verlag, 1930), 80–100; Idem., *Jewish Self-Hate*, trans. Peter C. Appelbaum (New York and Oxford: Berghahn Books, 2021), 51–64; Immanuel Kant (1724–1804), influential German philosopher in the Age of Enlightenment. In his doctrine of transcendental idealism, he argued that space, time, and causation are mere sensibilities; "things-in-themselves" exist, but their nature is unknowable; Johann Gottlieb Fichte (1762–1814), German philosopher and founding figure of the philosophical movement known as German idealism.

29 Jakob Wassermann (1873–1934), German novelist and writer of Jewish descent. *Das Dich* (the You, acc.) is untranslatable in English.

30 Charles Darwin (1809–1882), English naturalist geologist and biologist. best known for his contributions to the science of evolution and his book *The Origin of Species*. Thomas Carlyle (1795–1881), British historian, satirical writer, essayist, translator, philosopher, mathematician, and teacher. Lessing's assertion that Carlyle was England's greatest philosopher is ridiculous, but based on Carlyle's acceptance of the blue flower myth.

31 Lessing is referring to the last paragraph of Goethe's Faust (part 2);

Alles Vergängliche
Ist nur ein Gleichnis;
Das Unzulängliche,

Hier wird's Ereignis;
Das Unbeschreibliche,
Hier ist's getan;
Das Ewig-Weibliche
Zieht uns hinan.
(All things corruptible
Are but a parable;
Earth's insufficiency
Here finds fulfilment;
Here the ineffable,
Wins life through love;
Eternal womanhood
Leads us above.)

Lessing is being disingenuous. Rivers of ink have been spilled over these noble lines, but their precise remains obscure. The "eternal feminine" lies above, not below. In the last line of *The Divine Comedy*, Dante Alighieri (c. 1265–1321) calls God "the love that moves the sun and the other stars."

32   *Ich.*

33   *Das Nibelungenlied.*

34   In Norse mythology, Gerðr is a jötunn, goddess, and the wife of the god Freyr. Gerðr (Gerda, Erda) is commonly theorized to be a goddess associated with the earth.

35   Baldur, Norse god of light and purity, a son of Odin and Frigg, known for his beauty and near-invulnerability.

36   Untranslatable: *Ihr, Du.* Colloquial second person plural and singular, respectively.

About the Author

Theodor Lessing (1872–1933), was a German-Jewish philosopher. He taught at Hanover Technical College until right-wing student protests forced him to leave in 1926, after which he worked as an independent scholar and journalist. He fled to Czechoslovakia in early March 1933. In the summer of 1933, he took part in the Prague Zionist Conference, and planned to open a boarding school with his wife in Marienbad. At the same time, the Nazi press spread rumors of a large reward on Lessing's head. On August 30, 1933, he was shot and killed in his Marienbad apartment by two National Socialists. His assassination by the Nazis was the first political murder of an opponent to the Nazi regime outside of Germany, and caused worldwide indignation.

About the Editor/Translator

Peter C. Appelbaum, M.D., Ph.D., is Emeritus Professor of Pathology, Pennsylvania State University College of Medicine. After more than four decades in infectious disease research, Dr. Appelbaum is spending his retirement years writing and translating books on modern-day Jewish military history. Most recently, he translated and edited Theodor Lessing's *Jewish Self-Hate* (Berghahn Books, 2021). He is the author of *Loyalty Betrayed* and *Loyal Sons* (Vallentine-Mitchell, 2014), and *Habsburg Sons* (Academic Studies Press, 2022). Together with James Scott, he has translated an anthology of war essays and poems by Kurt Tucholsky (*Prayer after the Slaughter*, Berlinica, 2015) and *Broken Carousel: German Jewish Soldier-Poets of the Great War* (Stone Tower Books, 2017). He is also the translator/editor of *Jewish Tales of the Great*

War (Stone Tower Books, 2017). Dr. Appelbaum has also translated Avidgor Hameiri's *Of Human Carnage—Odessa 1918–1920* (Black Widow Press and Stone Tower Press, 2020), *The Great Madness* (Black Widow Press and Stone Tower Press, 2021), *Voyage into Savage Europe* (Academic Studies Press, 2020), and *Hell on Earth* by Avigdor Hameiri into English from the original Hebrew for the first time (Wayne State University Press, 2017). For that work, he was the recipient of the TLS-Risa Domb/Porjes Prize for Hebrew-English Translation for 2019.